DESERT KING, DOCTOR DADDY

BY
MEREDITH WEBBER

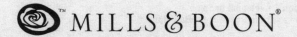

MILLS & BOON

First published in Great Britain 2010
Harlequin Mills & Boon Limited,
Eton House, 18-24 Paradise Road, Richmond, Surrey TW9 1SR

© Meredith Webber 2010

ISBN: 978 0 263 87689 5

Harlequin Mills & Boon policy is to use papers that are natural, renewable and recyclable products and made from wood grown in sustainable forests. The logging and manufacturing process conform to the legal environmental regulations of the country of origin.

Printed and bound in Spain
by Litografia Rosés, S.A., Barcelona

Yusef walked quietly along the dimly lit corridor, for he couldn't rest without seeing his little daughter, no matter how late the hour. He had not been here when she was born, and for that he carried guilt with him every day.

Pushing open the door, he saw light fall on red hair, and Yusef could only stare in disbelief, for there, on a mat on the floor, lay Gemma, her fiery red hair splayed across the pillow, her clothes dishevelled and creased. But her arms were around his daughter, who was snuggled close into Gemma's body.

His instinct was to wake the visitor, to tell her this wasn't her place. Yet why seeing her there should anger him, when all he should be feeling was gratitude, he didn't know.

Or did he? Wasn't it the stirring of his body, the shamefulness of such a reaction, that had angered him?

But as he watched the sleeping woman, with his child in her arms, desire departed, to be repla **a**
ind

Meredith Webber says of herself, 'Some years ago, I read an article which suggested that Mills and Boon were looking for new Medical™ Romance authors. I had one of those "I can do that" moments, and gave it a try. What began as a challenge has become an obsession—though I do temper the "butt on seat" career of writing with dirty but healthy outdoor pursuits, fossicking through the Australian Outback in search of gold or opals. Having had some success in all of these endeavours, I now consider I've found the perfect lifestyle.'

Recent titles by the same author:

DESERT KING, DOCTOR DADDY

CHAPTER ONE

SHE was almost done. The place shone—well, as much as an old terrace house in the inner city could shine. Magazines in the waiting room were neatly stacked, the toys tucked into toy boxes, the consulting rooms tidy, treatment rooms gleaming, crisp white paper on the examination tables. Flowers for the kitchen table, that's all she needed then she could change and be ready for the arrival of the Mystery Benefactor.

His donations had become so important over the last two years that Gemma couldn't help but think of him in capital letters. She grabbed a pair of scissors and headed out the door, knowing from the perfumed air that the valiant old mock orange tree on the eastern side of the house must be in flower again. A few sprays would lift the kitchen—the only room in the old house that hadn't benefited from the centre's extra income.

'Lady, lady!'

She was on the top step when she heard the call and turned to see a young man all but carrying a heavily pregnant woman along the footpath.

'Help me!' the man cried out again, but Gemma was already on her way towards him, the black limousine pulling up outside ignored in her haste to get to the couple.

Reaching them, she hooked her arm around the woman's waist to take her weight on one side, and recognised the beautiful features—Aisha, a young Somali woman who had stopped her antenatal visits two months ago, refusing to return to the Women's Centre in spite of repeated requests that she come in.

And now she had so, whatever the circumstances, Gemma welcomed her warmly.

'Aisha, it is good to see you. Are the pains bad? Have you been able to time them?'

Gemma kept talking, hoping her voice would reassure the labouring woman.

They'd reached the steps and as Gemma wondered how to make the journey up them easy for her patient, a tall, dark stranger appeared at her side.

'Go ahead and hold the door open, I will lift her,' he ordered, but he spoke with such authority that Gemma not only went ahead and opened the door but continued on into the house, opening a door to the treatment room as well.

The stranger set his burden down on the examination table but the woman screamed and lunged and would have fallen if the young man accompanying her hadn't caught her.

'Floor, she wants floor,' he said.

That was okay with Gemma. She'd delivered babies on the floor before today, but the young man's presence was nearly as puzzling as the stranger's. Somali men, in her experience, were rarely present at their baby's birth. It was an all-women affair. And surely the beautifully suited, slightly severe-looking man who'd appeared couldn't be her M.B.—she'd been picturing a doddering octogenarian, not a suave, handsome fashion plate who couldn't be a day over forty.

Not that there was time to question either of the men. Squatting on the floor beside Aisha, one arm around her, sup-

porting her, the other on her belly, Gemma felt the strong
contractions and although the woman was doing no more
than making tiny mewling noises, Gemma knew she must
be in agony.

'What's been happening?' she asked the young man.

'The women who help, the doula and the other women who
promise to help, they say baby die and they walk away from
my Aisha. I bring her here.'

Gemma nodded her approval but her hands were feeling
for the baby's position now, and she was discovering exactly
why the women who'd been going to help Aisha had opted
out. It was a breech presentation, and the baby was too far
down the birth canal for her to try to turn it. The problem was,
she reflected as she squatted on the floor seeking the degree
of cervical dilatation, that a baby's bottom didn't provide as
effective a wedge as a head to force the birth canal open and
the cervix to dilate.

'You must help her,' the young man implored. 'She has
suffered too much already, my Aisha. You must get her baby
out. It is for the baby she lives.'

'He is not exaggerating,' the other man, the stranger, said,
as if he was tuned into the labouring woman's thoughts. 'You
must save the baby.'

Startled by what sounded very like another order,
Gemma glanced across at the stranger who was squatting
now, for all his immaculate clothing, beside the woman,
talking soothingly to her in some language Gemma didn't
understand.

Somali?

He caught her eye and said, 'I will help. I will monitor her
pulse and breathing, you do what you have to do.'

Did he know what she would have to do? Know that freeing

the little infant legs before easing them out and delivering the baby would not be comfortable for Aisha?

'We'll manage,' she said, her heart in her mouth because she knew it wasn't going to be easy. Fortunately, it wasn't the first time she'd had to deliver a baby at the centre so she was now prepared with a sterile bundle on hand—everything she'd need, and wrappings for the infant as well. She spread a thick paper mat beneath the woman, who had insisted on squatting as soon as Gemma had finished the examination. But squatting wasn't going to work, so Gemma, with the stranger's help, eased her backwards and administered some local pain relief before making a small incision. After that it was a straightforward breech delivery, feeling for a leg and releasing it, then another scrawny leg, gentle pressure until the buttocks were revealed, a slight turn of the shoulder, her finger finding the baby's mouth to keep its head in position for the final push.

And through it all the two men talked to and encouraged the woman, who still made no more fuss than the occasional mew of discomfort.

Gemma suctioned the tiny boy and as he gave his first cry, she handed him to his father, who pressed the little one against his wife's chest, the umbilical cord still trailing.

Gemma smiled at the picture, her heart as always gladdened by the miracle of birth, especially gladdened by this one. Here were two young people starting a new life in a strange land—and now they had a child to enrich their future.

'Do you want to cut the cord?' she asked the young man.

'Do Australian men do that?' he asked, amazement widening his shining black eyes.

'A lot of them do,' she said, but when Gemma handed him the scissors, Aisha cried out in protest, then spoke urgently in her language.

'Let me handle this,' the stranger said, and something in his voice made Gemma turn her attention to the baby, wrapping a cloth around him as she lay against his mother's breast.

'He's beautiful,' Gemma told her, hoping her smile would translate the words. 'Truly beautiful.'

With the final stage of delivery finished, Gemma cleaned up her patient then left the little family on the floor of the treatment room, nodding her head towards the door so the stranger followed.

'They need time alone and I need time to figure out what to do next,' she explained. Then she looked at him—really looked. Stared, in fact, at mesmeric black eyes set in a swarthy skin, dark eyebrows arched across the obsidian eyes, while his nose was finely boned, leading the gaze down towards lips rimmed in paler skin, not too full but suggesting a sensuality that made her skin tingle.

Skin tingle? It must be because she'd been nervous about the visit that she was reacting this way!

'Mr Akkedi? I'm assuming that's who you are?'

He moved his head in such an infinitesimal nod that if she hadn't been staring at him she wouldn't have noticed.

'I'm sorry not to greet you properly. Even now, I can't really spend time with you. Aisha should be in hospital, or at least somewhere she and the baby can be cared for. I need to get hold of our translator as she'll know—'

'Can you not even pause to be pleased with the wonder of birth? To enjoy the achievement of delivering a healthy baby?'

It wasn't exactly criticism but it felt like it to Gemma.

'How can I be pleased,' she protested, 'when she risked so much? And when she has suffered unnecessarily? Somehow we must learn to overcome the fears some women have about visiting doctors, we must do better—'

She broke off, shook her head at her own regrets, and smiled at him.

'Of course I should pause,' she admitted, 'for surely the birth of a child is a reaffirmation of all that is good in humanity, no matter what has gone before.'

Yusef stared at her—at the smile that had transformed her face. She was a mess, this woman with the wild red hair escaping from the bounds of a scarf, clad in a faded T-shirt and jeans worn by age rather than fashion. Shadows of tiredness lay dark beneath her pale green eyes, almost translucent, like the new spring leaves on the almond trees at home. Yet her smile made her face come alive, as if all the tiny golden freckles on her skin were sparking with electricity, causing a glow.

Was he mad? Standing in this shabby house, staring at a woman, when so much work awaited him at home? He had to talk to her, professionally. Had to explain his plans.

Not that he could when she was obviously still thinking of the couple and their baby. Her smile faded and worry etched lines in her forehead.

'Surely time, and perhaps the experience of those like Aisha, will overcome those fears,' he said, wanting to see Gemma Murray smile again.

'I keep hoping that's the case,' she said.

Yusef nodded, although the doubt in her voice puzzled him. Everything he had learned about this woman and the centre she had set up built a picture of someone who really cared not only about her patients but about treating them with respect for their culture and heritage. As for fear, how could she think the patients might fear her when he had seen at first hand her kindness to the young couple, her empathy and understanding as she'd delivered their child?

He watched her cross the hall, her mind no doubt on her

patient, but as she passed the front door it opened and another young woman, also from her looks Somali, came bursting in.

'Aisha?' she asked, and Gemma Murray, for although introductions hadn't been completed Yusef knew it must be her, replied.

'Sahra, I was about to call you. Aisha's in there,' she said, pointing to the room, 'with her husband and new son. Will you talk to them, Sahra, and sort out what's best to do for both of them now? This is Mr Akkedi, our benefactor. I have to talk to him but I'll be in the kitchen if you need me.'

She led the way towards the back of the house and Yusef followed her, then looked with distaste at the collection of old chairs that surrounded an equally old Formica table.

'You do not use the money for some decent furniture?' he asked, then realised his mistake for the woman had turned back towards him with a frown.

'New tables and chairs for the kitchen or an ultrasound machine—there's no choice, you know. Actually, a new table and chairs would cost much less but there's always something more important. Would you like a coffee?'

He glanced at the tin of instant coffee on the kitchen bench and gave an inward shudder, although he'd drunk the same brand when he'd been working in Africa, and had survived.

'No, thank you.'

A man who only drank real coffee, Gemma surmised. He was reminding her more and more of her grandfather! Well, that was too bad! She put on the kettle, explaining as she did so that she needed caffeine, and needed it now!

'The young woman, Aisha, was a patient?' the man asked, and she sighed, poured boiling water over the coffee powder, added sugar and sat down.

'Aisha came to us early in her pregnancy. She knew her

delivery might be difficult and we discussed all options, including Caesarean.'

She took a sip of coffee and risked another look at the man, who was now sitting cautiously on the edge of a chair across the table from her. A table without mock orange flowers to brighten it or perfume the room.

'You spoke to her in her own language. Do you know Somalia?' she asked him, thinking she might have less to explain if he'd been in the country.

'I worked there in a refugee camp for some years,' he said, surprising her so much the coffee went down the wrong way and she coughed and snorted.

'I am dressed for business today,' he said, ultra-cool but reading the cause of her surprise with ease. 'Neither should you judge by appearances!'

'Of course,' Gemma managed realising she'd been put firmly in her place. 'But I asked because I wondered if you knew much of their customs and beliefs, which obviously you would. Perhaps not the women, though. They want big families, many children…'

'And they worry that a Caesar will prevent them having as many as they want?'

Gemma nodded.

'Not all of them, but some. Perhaps that's why I've seen little of Aisha lately, why I feel I've failed her.'

'She came to you when she needed help, that is not failure.' He sounded so stern she had to look at him again, although she'd been trying to avoid doing that, as looking at him was causing some very strange reactions in her body.

'I suppose so.'

'Of course so. You cannot make patients come to you!'

'You know this?'

'I am a surgeon—or was a surgeon. Working with refugees, you try to help wherever you can and whoever you can, but you cannot help those who do not wish to be helped.'

The dark eyes held shadows of pain so deep Gemma wondered just what horrors he must have seen, but every instinct told her he was a very private man and she shouldn't—couldn't—pry.

'Is it because of your work with the refugees that you have put so much money into our centre?'

'That, and other reasons,' he said, his voice suggesting he was still lost in memory.

Fortunately, Sahra appeared at that moment.

'I will take Aisha and her baby home to my place. My mother will take care of them both and if they are there and either of them have problems I will take them to the hospital.'

'Fantastic,' Gemma told her, then turned to her visitor. 'This is Sahra. She, too, is from Somalia but has been here longer, going to school then university and getting her nursing and specialist midwifery qualifications, so as well as translating for those of us who find it hard to learn the language, she understands the best ways to help the women.'

The stranger stood up and held out his hand.

'Sheikh Yusef Akkedi,' he said, and to Gemma's amazement, the usually undemonstrative Sahra simply took his hand, sank low into a curtsey and kissed his fingers.

'But you are famous, Your Highness,' she said, still on her knees. 'My family get papers from home, we read of you and see your name, learn of your elevation to be the leader of your country. I did not recognise you immediately—you have no beard now.'

She released his hand and put her own hand to her cheek,

then, even through her dark skin, Gemma saw her blush as the visitor helped her to her feet.

'I am honoured to have met you,' Sahra added, then hurried out the door, almost falling over herself in her confusion.

Confusion resounded in Gemma's mind and body.

'I'd better check on the couple and the baby but I'll be right back,' she told the man—a sheikh? A highness?

She'd heard of the incredible wealth of sheikhs, but Sahra curtseying like that—is that how *she* should have been treating him?

Gemma followed Sahra, needing time to sort out why this man's status should come as such a shock to her. Surely she wasn't worried about who donated money. It didn't matter as long as the centre could continue its work.

Aisha was on her feet, cradling the swaddled baby in her arms, her husband proudly supporting his wife and child.

'You are sure you don't want to take her to the hospital so both of them can be checked out?' Gemma asked the young man.

'No hospital,' he said, so firmly Gemma suspected they'd made the decision some time ago. 'We go with Sahra, and Aisha's mother will help Sahra's mother care for the baby while Aisha rests.'

Gemma led them out but couldn't let them go without having one more look at the tiny infant, so perfect in every way, his ebony skin shining, his dark eyes gazing unfocusedly at the world into which he had been born. Aisha let go of the swaddled bundle long enough for Gemma to hold him, and her arms felt the familiar heavy ache, not of loss but of dreams unfulfilled…

'Definitely miraculous,' she admitted to the sheikh, who had appeared at the back of the hall to see the little family off.

Yusef watched her as she handed back the baby, reluctantly

it seemed to him, then opened the door to let the group out. What had made this woman, who could be earning big money as a specialist in a city practice, take on the frustrating and often, he imagined, impossible task, of providing medical care for immigrant women and their children?

That she also went beyond straight medical care, he knew from the reports he had read. She had a part-time psychologist on staff, and ran various clubs and get-togethers for the women who visited the centre. She had dragooned a dentist into service once a fortnight and a paediatrician visited once a month to see the children of the women who used the centre.

He studied her as she spoke to the nurse, seeing a profile with a high forehead beneath the red hair, a long thin nose, neatly curved lips and a chin with a small dimple that saved it from being downright stubborn. A handsome woman, not beautiful but attractive in the real sense of the word—attracting glances, he was sure, wherever she went.

Yet she made nothing of herself, scraping the vibrant hair back into a tight knot and swathing it with a scarf, although he doubted it stayed tidy long, and wearing no make-up to hide the little golden freckles most women he knew would consider blemishes.

She was back inside, shutting the door behind her, and she must have seen his visual check because she gave a shrug and said, 'It *is* Sunday morning and I was in the centre, making sure all the paperwork was in order for your visit, and that the place was clean. I do have some decent clothes to change into if you've time to wait.'

Yusef had to smile.

'Of course you mustn't change for me. Was my study of you so obvious?' he asked, as she led the way back to the kitchen.

'Not as obvious as the look on your face when you were wondering why on earth I do the job I do,' she said, and Yusef, who, like all his people, prided himself on keeping all his thoughts and emotions hidden behind a bland face, felt affronted.

And she read that emotion too, chuckling, more to herself than to him, then explaining.

'I deal with women who are past masters at hiding their emotions behind the blankest of expressions. Reading their faces, the slightest changes in their expressions, helps me to know when I've pushed too far, or reached ground too delicate to tread.'

It was the simple truth, for he too could read people, but the mystery remained.

'And why *do* you do the job you do?'

She slumped down in a chair and picked up her coffee, which by now must be lukewarm as well as revolting.

'Because I love it?'

'You make that a question. Are you not sure, or are you asking me if I'd believe that answer?'

She glanced his way then shrugged her shoulders.

'I do love it, but it wasn't because I doubted you'd believe me. I think the question you were asking was more than that, because how could I possibly have known how much pleasure it would give me before I began the centre?'

'Yet it gives you grief, as well,' Yusef persisted, although he was coming close to personal ground—ground he rarely trod with either men or women, particularly not with women he didn't know. 'I saw your face as you examined Aisha.'

Gemma studied him in silence and he could almost hear the debate going on inside her head. Would she answer him or brush him off? In the end, she did answer, but perhaps it was a brush-off as well.

'Terrible things happen to innocent people, we all know that, our news broadcasts are full of it every day. A war here, a famine there, floods and earthquakes and tidal waves—these things we can't control, but what we can do is help pick up the pieces. Some of those pieces wash up on the shores of my country, and it gives me more joy than grief if I can help them.'

Yusef heard the truth of what she said in every word and although what he wanted back at home was not someone to pick up scraps left by disasters, well, not entirely, he *did* want someone with the empathy this woman felt and the understanding she had for marginalised people. His country was changing, and many tribal groups that had once roamed freely over all the desert before those lands had had borders and names were now having to live within the boundaries of a particular country—many of them in his country.

These people saw the money flowing into his country, and the life it could provide, and wanted some of it for themselves, but their arrival was putting stresses on basic infrastructure like hospitals and clinics. This, in itself, was causing difficulties and unrest, something Yusef wanted to put a stop to as early as possible. He knew the tribal women made the decisions for the family, and that it would take someone special to help them settle comfortably in his land. He'd suspected, from the first time he'd heard of this women's centre in Sydney that the woman who ran it might be the person he was seeking.

'You are committed, but your staff? Do they also feel as you do?'

She smiled at him, and again it seemed as if a light had gone on behind the fine, pale skin of her face, illuminating all the tiny freckles so she shone like an oil lamp in the desert darkness. Something shifted in his chest, as if his heart had tugged at its moorings, but he knew such things didn't happen—a momentary fibrillation, nothing more. Stress, no doubt, brought on by the task that lay ahead of him.

'I could walk out of here tomorrow and nothing would change,' she assured him proudly. '*That* is probably my greatest achievement. Although everyone likes to believe he or she is indispensable, it's certainly not the case here. My staff believe, as I do, that we must treat the women who come here without judging them in any way, and that we must be sensitive to their cultural beliefs and customs and as far as possible always act in ways that won't offend them.'

She paused then gave a rueful laugh.

'Oh, we make mistakes, and sometimes we let our feelings show—I must have today for you to have picked up on my anxiety when I examined Aisha. But generally we manage and the women have come to trust us.'

'Except when it comes to a Caesarean birth?'

She gave a little shrug.

'You're right. No matter how hard we try to convince them that they can have more children after a Caesarean, they don't believe us.'

She sighed.

'There's no perfect world.'

Yusef took a deep breath, thinking about all she had covered in not so many words. He knew the trauma many women suffered in the refugee camps. Of course this woman—Gemma Murray—would feel their pain, yet she continued to do her job.

He now reflected on the other thing she'd said. She could leave tomorrow and the centre's work would continue.

Was this true?

* * *

What was he thinking now? Gemma wondered.

Had she made a fool of herself talking about the centre the way she had?

Been too emotional?

Gemma watched the man across the table, his gaze fixed on some point beyond her shoulder, obviously thinking but about what she had no clue for his face was totally impassive now.

'*Would* you leave tomorrow?' he asked.

CHAPTER TWO

THE question was so totally unexpected, Gemma could only stare at him, and before she could formulate a reply, he spoke again.

'And your second house, would you be equally confident leaving it?'

She could feel the frown deepening on her forehead but still couldn't answer, although she knew she had to—knew there was something important going on here, even if she didn't understand it.

Think, brain, think!

'None of your money has gone into the second house,' she said, then realised she'd sounded far too defensive and tried to laugh it off. 'Sorry, but I wasn't sure you knew about it.'

He had a stillness about him, this man who had virtually saved their service, and perhaps because he'd let emotion show earlier and had regretted it, his face was now impossible to read.

'I know of its existence,' her visitor said, 'but not of how it came to be. It seems to me you had enough—is the expression "on your plate"?—without taking on more waifs and strays.'

Was it his stillness that made her fidget with the sugar basin on the table? She wasn't usually a fidget, but pushing it around

and rearranging the salt and pepper grinders seemed to ease
her tension as she tried to explain. Actually, anything was
preferable to looking at him as she answered, because looking
at him was causing really weird sensations in her body.

She was finding him attractive?

Surely not, although he was undeniably attractive…

She moved the pepper grinder back to where it had been
and concentrated on business.

'The sign on our front door, although fairly discreet, does
say Women's Centre, and with our inner-city position, I
suppose it was inevitable that some women who were not im-
migrants would turn up here. Not often, in the beginning, but
one in particular, an insulin-dependent diabetic, began to
come regularly, and sometimes bring a friend, or recommend
us to another woman.'

'These are women of the streets you talk of?'

The pepper grinder was in the wrong place again and
Gemma shifted it, then looked up at her questioner.

'I don't know about your country—or even what country
you call home—but here a lot of people with mental health
problems or addictions end up living on the streets. The government, church and charity organisations all do what they
can, and homeless people have the same access to free
hospital care at public hospitals, but…'

What did she not want to say? Yusef watched her restless
hands, moving things on the table, the tiny golden freckles on
her long slim fingers fascinating him. Everything about this
woman was fascinating him, which in itself should be a
warning to find someone else. The last complication he
needed in his life right now was to be attracted to a woman,
particularly one he was intending to employ.

Yet his eyes kept straying to her vivid hair, her freckled

skin, the way her pale lips moved as she spoke—which she was doing now so he should concentrate.

'Sometimes there is an element of judgement in the treatment of these women, or if not judgement then a genuine desire to help them, but to help them by changing their way of life.'

She tucked her hands onto her lap where they couldn't fiddle—and he could no longer see them—and looked directly at him.

'I am not saying this is a bad thing. I am not saying that organisations dedicated to helping these people shouldn't exist, it is just that sometimes all they want is a diagnosis of some small problem and, where necessary, a prescription. Sometimes they don't want to be helped in other ways, or cured of an addiction, or to change their lives.'

Was she so naïve? Could she not see that a lot of the organisations set up for these people were funded on the basis that they did attempt to change lives? It was their duty to at least try!

'But surely a drug addict should be helped to fight his or her addiction?' he asked, and watched her closely, trying to fathom where her totally non-judgemental attitude had come from. Trying to focus on the discussion they were having, not on the effect she was having on his body.

'Of course,' she said, 'and as I said there are plenty of places willing to help in that way. If someone asks for that kind of help we refer them on, but our—our charter, I suppose you could say, is purely medical. We are a medical centre for people who are intimidated by the public health system, or for some other reason do not wish to use it.'

'And for that you bought a house?'

Defiance flashed in the pale eyes. Would desire heat them in the same way?

Yusef groaned, but inwardly. It had to be because he'd

been so busy these last six months, too busy for anything but the briefest social encounters with women, that his body was behaving the way it was. Not only his body, but his mind, it seemed.

'I live in that house,' she said, the words carrying an icy edge. 'It is my home. And if I choose to turn the upstairs into a flat and the downstairs into a surgery, then that is my business.'

Ah, so she had the fire that supposedly accompanied the colour of her hair—fire and ice…

'I am not criticising. I think it is admirable, and that brings me back to my original question. Could you walk away from these services you have set up?'

Gemma studied him, suspicion coiling in her stomach, keeping company with the other stuff that was happening there every time she looked at this man. It couldn't be attraction, for all that he was the best looking man she'd ever seen. She didn't do attraction any more. Attraction led to such chaos it was easier to avoid it.

'Why are you asking that?' she demanded, probably too demandingly but he had her rattled. 'Are you implying that if I left, the staff I've trained, the staff who work here because they hold the same beliefs I do, would turn the services into something else? And if so, would you withdraw your funding? Is that where your questions are leading?'

Fire! It was sparking from her now, but he had to concentrate—had to think whether now was the time to talk of the new venture. Probably not. She was too suspicious of him.

'You may be sure of my contributions to your service continuing, even increasing,' he said. 'Though perhaps now would be a good time for me to look at more of the facilities than the treatment room you used for Aisha. Perhaps you can tell me what else is needed.' He stood up, relieved to get off the uncomfortable and not totally, he suspected, clean chair. 'Apart,' he added with a smile, 'from some new kitchen furniture.'

Gemma was sorry he'd smiled. She'd been okay denying the attraction right up until then, but the smile sneaked through a crack in her defences and weakened not only her resistance but the muscles in her chest so she found it hard to breathe normally and had to remind herself—in, out, in, out!

'A tour, good,' she said, standing up and all but running out of the kitchen—anything to escape the man's presence. Although he'd still be with her, but surely explaining the use to which they put the various rooms would take her mind off the attraction.

She led him through the ground-floor rooms first, then up the stairs to where she'd had two small bedrooms altered to make a larger meeting room.

'We have playgroups for the children here,' she said. 'It's wonderful to see them all singing nursery rhymes in English, and chattering to each other in a medley of languages that they all seem to understand. In the beginning the mothers usually come along as well, but as they grow in confidence themselves, they will leave the children and go off for a coffee. And as they get to know each other, they make arrangements to meet at places other than the centre, in a park at weekends, with their extended families. The centre has become a kind of cultural crossroads, and that pleases me enormously.'

Talking about the centre was good—Gemma was so wholehearted about what the place had achieved that she didn't have to pretend enthusiasm. Neither did she have to look at her visitor—well, not more than an occasional glance.

'And the other rooms on this floor?'

'A bedroom and bathroom for on-duty staff. I was on-duty last night and although I only live next door I do a night shift here once a month.'

Now she did look at him.

'We need a doctor on hand for obstetric emergencies. It doesn't seem to matter how careful we are in our antenatal clinics and how often we take pregnant women to the hospital and show them the birthing suites, nurseries and maternity wards, some, like Aisha, will not go to a hospital.'

He nodded as if he understood, and the haunted look was back on his face, as if he'd seen things in hospitals in other places that he'd rather not remember.

She wanted to reach out and touch his arm, to offer comfort, though for what she didn't know, but she shrugged off the silly notion as he evidently shrugged off his memories, asking, 'And is there someone on duty in the other house?'

Gemma shook her head.

'The other house is strictly week-days, day and evening appointments although most of the patients who attend don't bother with appointments. From time to time, someone turns up here late at night or on a weekend, but it's rare. I think the women who use the service consider it a bit special so they are reluctant to abuse it.'

She had no sooner finished speaking than the doorbell peeled, echoing through the empty rooms downstairs.

'Surely not another emergency birth,' she muttered as she headed down the steps. She could hear her visitor coming down behind her but her focus was on the door, beyond which she could hear shrill wails.

Gemma flung open the door to find two women grappling on the doorstep. The air smelt of old wet wool and blood, which was liberally splattered over both of them. As Gemma moved closer she thought she saw the flash of a knife, then she was thrust aside by a powerful arm and the man who'd followed her stepped past her, putting his arms around one of the women and lifting her cleanly off the step.

'Drop the knife,' he ordered, not loudly but with such authority the woman in his arms obeyed instantly, a battered, rusty carving knife falling to the ground.

Gemma scooped it up and shoved it behind the umbrella stand in the foyer, temporarily out of harm's way, then she turned her attention to the woman who had had collapsed onto the floor just inside the door—Jackie, one of the older women who used the medical services at the house next door.

The sheikh—after his authoritative intervention Gemma found herself thinking of him that way—was talking soothingly to the attacker, whom he had settled into a chair.

'What happened, Jackie?' Gemma asked as she bent over the woman on the floor. Jackie didn't reply but Gemma could see blood oozing between the fingers of her left hand, which were clasped tightly on her upper right arm.

'Touched my things. She touched my things,' Bristow, the second woman, roared from the other side of the room.

'Jackie wouldn't do that,' Gemma said, turning to face the attacker, who was huddled in the chair, her damp and wrinkled layers of cardigans and coats making her look like an insect that had sunk back into its chrysalis. The sheikh stood beside her, perhaps perplexed by her retreat. 'She's your friend,' Gemma added. 'She knows not to touch your things.'

Gemma helped Jackie back to her feet and half carried her into the treatment room, the sheikh joining her and lifting Jackie onto the examination table. This time the patient didn't object and Gemma was able to unfasten Jackie's fingers and move enough clothing to see the long, deep gash in Jackie's arm.

'She needs to go to hospital—it's deep, there could be nerve and ligament damage.'

The sheikh was right behind her, and Gemma turned, puzzled by his instant diagnosis.

'I told you I was a surgeon,' he said, but his voice was drowned out by Jackie's cries.

'No hospital, no hospital. I can't go to hospital,' she wailed, and Gemma turned towards the visitor.

'There are reasons,' she said quietly.

'Then I'll do it,' he said. 'You can get me what I need—I assume you have sutures—and assist me. Her friend will be all right?'

Gemma didn't know how to answer that. She'd known Bristow for over a year and never seen any signs of violence, but now this had happened, who knew what the little woman might do?

'You'll do it yourself?'

It didn't seem right. The man was a benefactor—not to mention a sheikh and apparently a highness, although that really wasn't the point. Surely sheikhs had as much right to be surgeons as anyone else. It just seemed…unseemly somehow that the man in the beautiful suit should be—

'Shall I look for myself to see what's available?' Curt words! The man had tied his handkerchief around Jackie's arm to slow the bleeding and was obviously getting impatient.

Gemma hurried towards the cabinet. Jackie's tremors were getting stronger and though a quick glance had shown that Bristow was still sitting on a chair in the foyer; if she disappeared further into her coat she'd be nothing but a bundle of rags. And, Gemma knew from experience, she wouldn't emerge to answer questions or even move from the chair for some considerable time.

'Here,' she told the visitor, unlocking the cabinet and piling all she thought he might need onto a tray. Local anaesthetic, a bottle of antiseptic liquid, swabs, sutures and dressings joined a couple of pairs of gloves.

'A gown—there must be a plain gown,' she muttered, but as hard as she flipped through the folded gowns on the bottom shelf there was nothing that was really suitable for such a man.

'Anything will do,' he said, calling to her from the sink at the corner where he'd stripped off his coat, rolled up his shirt-sleeves and was now scrubbing his hands.

'It'll have to,' Gemma muttered to herself but the largest gown she could find, one she often wore herself, had bunny rabbits hopping gleefully all over it.

Yusef grimaced as she held it up for him but, wanting to save his shirt and suit trousers, he slid his arms into it and let her tie it behind him, concentrating on the job ahead, not his awareness of the woman who'd slipped her arms around him to get the ties. He snapped on gloves and returned to his patient. She was trembling, but whether from nerves or from pain or from a pre-existing condition he had no idea.

All he could do was try to soothe her, talking quietly to her, knowing that the sound of a human voice was sometimes more important than the words it spoke. The gash on her arm was deep and he worried that it might be infected.

'Will she take a course of antibiotics?' He turned so he could quietly ask the question of Gemma without upsetting the patient.

'Probably not, but if we give her a tetanus and antibiotic shot today, that might hold off any infection. We can try to get her back to have the stitches removed.'

Yusef understood what she was saying—that these women might not return to the surgery for months, but if Jackie could be convinced to come back for some reason then they might be able to give her more antibiotics.

He swabbed and stitched, talking all the time, feeling Jackie growing calmer under his prattle. And it was prattle. He talked of a wound he'd had as a young boy, out in the desert, a wound one of the women of the family had stitched with sewing thread. Then, for good measure, he told her of the infection that had set in and how his father had told him he'd lose his arm if he didn't take some medicine. This last part wasn't quite true, and he read disbelief in Gemma's eyes, but she seemed to understand his motive and went along with it.

But having Gemma so close to him was accelerating all the physical impulses his body was experiencing, and adding to his belief that taking this woman to his country might not be the best of ideas.

Except that she was so exactly what he needed! What the service he hoped to set up needed.

'I bet there's no infection scar,' she muttered to him, as they left Jackie, wound stitched and dressed, on the table and went to wash their hands.

'You're right, although the sewing thread part was true. In point of fact, my father was in the city at the time, but when he heard, he sent a helicopter and had me flown out, flying in a surgeon from Singapore of all places to ensure the wound would heal as cleanly as possible.'

Gemma shook her head. The man must inhabit a world so different from her own it seemed like another planet. But other planet or not, he had been extremely helpful, and still could be.

'If you could help Jackie off the table, maybe offer her a cup of tea and something to eat, I'll talk to Bristow.'

He looked startled, as if no one had ever asked him to make tea for a street-person before, but then he smiled and crossed to Jackie's side, talking again—more stories?

Gemma found Bristow still huddled in the chair in the foyer. She squatted beside her.

'Talk to me,' she said, her voice quietly persuasive. 'Tell me what happened.'

Bristow's head inched out of the coat.

'Medicine, she tried to take my medicine. She take that and she die. I tell her she die.'

Tears began rolling down Bristow's cheeks, her rheumy eyes reddened by her anguish.

'You're right,' Gemma told her, patting the bundle of rags. 'It's okay. I understand and Jackie's going to be okay. Now, seeing you're here, let's go into my office and I'll check you out.'

'I need my knife.'

Gemma hesitated, then pulled the knife from behind the umbrella stand.

'I can't give it back to you,' she said gently, touching Bristow on the cheek. 'You must know that.'

Bristow's head dropped deeper into the bundle of coats and rags and Gemma felt so guilty she added, 'You don't really need it, Bristow. Jackie won't touch your things again.'

'My things outside. Must get my things.' Bristow had hopped off the chair and was bouncing up and down, her agitation increasing every second.

Gemma ushered her out, knowing the elderly woman wouldn't be settled until she had her old pram full of plastic bags of treasure with her again. They retrieved the pram, then she led Bristow into a consulting room and talked quietly to her, although she'd have loved to have been a fly on the wall in the kitchen. All she could hear was the faint murmur of the man's voice, but his presence in the old house unsettled Gemma as she talked Bristow out of her agitation, checked her blood sugar and assured her she'd done the right thing in not letting Jackie touch her insulin but gently chiding her for using the knife.

'She had to understand,' Bristow said, and Gemma shrugged, not wanting to agitate the woman again. Bristow was right, and even if her methods were a little extreme, Gemma was reasonably sure that Jackie would never touch the insulin again.

'So maybe now we can talk.'

Gemma shut the door on the ill-assorted pair and turned to find her visitor right behind her. He'd taken off the happy, hopping bunny wrap but hadn't put on his jacket, which he'd hung on the knob at the bottom of the stair banister. He'd also removed his tie and draped it over his coat, so, with his shirtsleeves rolled up and his collar unbuttoned, he looked a very different man from the one she'd met earlier that morning.

An even more attractive man!

And given the attraction, she should be seeing him off the premises as quickly as possible, but politeness—and his promise of even more donations—prevailed.

'I'm sorry we keep being interrupted, but it's lunchtime and Beth's just arrived to relieve me. Can I offer you some lunch? We can go up to my flat where we won't be disturbed, or do you have to be somewhere?'

Yusef thought of all the business he'd hoped to get done after his morning meeting at the centre, and all the reasons he shouldn't be spending more time in this woman's company, but so far he'd achieved nothing of his main purpose. He *had* to spend more time with her.

'Lunch sounds good but can't I take you somewhere?'

'Tempting though that sounds, I think we should get down

to business and we can hardly do that in a restaurant. Besides, I'm sure you're already way beyond the time you scheduled for this meeting, so it will be quicker and easier to eat next door.'

She ducked into one of the consulting rooms to speak to someone, then returned, a bundle of keys dangling from her fingers.

'Beth's another of the doctors on staff. She's done the O and G short course and hopes to go back to study next year to do a full specialty course. We've been lucky to get so many good quality staff, especially as the pay isn't nearly as much as they'd earn in private practice.'

She led the way outside, Yusef pausing to grab his jacket and tie, then down the steps and up the steps of the adjacent house, unlocking the bright red front door.

'The steps are a nuisance but we've a ramp at the side entrance next door, which makes it easier for mothers with prams and strollers.'

Was she nervous that her conversation sounded like anxious chatter? Yusef found himself wishing he knew her better so he could judge this reaction.

'The house is a twin of the one next door?' He was looking around a black and white tiled foyer, a wooden staircase curving up on the right, doors opening off the passageway on the left. He hung his discarded clothing on the banister again.

'Exactly the same, except that I've only one consulting and treatment room downstairs, and upstairs I've converted all the space into a small flat. Come on up.'

Gemma felt a shiver start at the top of her spine and travel down to her toes as she uttered the invitation. But why? She'd been attracted to men before, not often, admittedly, but it had happened. And there'd been handsome men, and wealthy men, and very ordinary men that had stirred something in her—but attraction had never felt like this. Never so instant, so physical, so—hot?

She unlocked the door into her flat, mentally chiding herself for not accepting the man's invitation to go out somewhere for lunch. Once he'd been into the flat, his image, she guessed, would haunt it.

Shaking her head at such fanciful thoughts, she waved him into the big room that was divided into functions by its furniture—living room, dining room and at the far end a small kitchen.

'Compact and functional,' he said, looking around but not taking an armchair in the living area, moving instead to the kitchen bench where he pulled out a stool and settled on it. 'And a coffee machine! Thank heavens. Do you do a strong espresso?'

Gemma turned the machine on and programmed it, setting a small cup under the spout. She felt uncomfortable now that she had such a luxury in her own home yet the kitchen-cum-tearoom in the centre was so poorly furnished. Embarrassment curled her toes.

'It was a present from a cousin,' she said. 'I could hardly give it away to the centre.'

Sheikh Yusef Akkedi, the highness, smiled at her.

'So defensive,' he teased, making the toe-curl far worse than it had been. 'Believe me, in my tent in Mogadishu, I treasured little comforts myself. Not a coffee machine but a small coffee pot I could put over a flame, and coffee grounds I hoarded like a miser.'

Gemma turned from where she was digging lettuce and tomatoes out of her refrigerator and stared at him.

'You mentioned Africa before, and I know of the wonderful work medical organisations do in such places, but—'

'But me?' he said, smiling again, although this time the

sadness was back in his eyes. 'You hear Sahra use the "highness" word and wonder what such a person is doing working with refugees?'

'Well, yes,' Gemma admitted, taking the little cup of espresso from the machine and passing it to him, being careful to set it down in front of him so their fingers didn't touch. It was bad enough having him close, but touching him? 'Even being a doctor,' she added, pulling herself together.

'The "highness" part is very recent,' her visitor replied, unaware of the confusion he was causing in her body. 'And totally unexpected. My oldest brother inherited the title from my father, but there are no strict guidelines of succession in my country. The current ruler chooses his successor, choosing someone he believes will follow in the way he has ruled. He might choose a brother or a cousin, although my father chose his eldest son. Unfortunately my brother didn't want the task. He is an aesthete and prefers to spend his life in spiritual learning and contemplation. He could not tell our father this for it would have disappointed him, but when my father died my brother relinquished the crown.'

'Passing it to you,' Gemma put in, wondering if there was an actual crown or if it was a figure of speech. She wondered about the country her visitor now ruled. There'd been no mention of it, but she knew it would be a long way off—way beyond her hope of ever reaching.

And that couldn't possibly be regret she was feeling…

Yusef moved his head, just slightly, indicating she'd guessed incorrectly. Was she interested or just making conversation? With women he could never tell, a gap in his education he put down to not having known his mother, although there'd been women aplenty in his life. Transient women, he considered them, there for a while but moving on, perhaps being forced to move on by his lack of commitment to them—his detachment—

'My brother intended passing the title to his next brother, the one above me, because that is how it would most easily have been done,' Yusef explained. 'But even before my father died that brother was working with foreign companies, bringing them in to search for oil, making treaties that would allow them access to whatever they discovered in return for favours for the country.'

The woman frowned at him.

'You sound as if you disapprove, but isn't that how the countries around yours have been able to go ahead? And hasn't oil made the people of those lands wealthy?'

'Of course it has, and what my business brother does is good—essential—and that is his life—his love,' Yusef told her, a little curtly, though why her pointing out the obvious about their wealth should worry him he didn't know. Maybe it was because her frown had disturbed him. 'But you must know that wealth is not everything. Wealth, as I said earlier, attracts more people to the country. My brother sees this as a good thing. He does not see the overcrowded schools and hospitals and clinics, the sick children and mothers who have suffered in childbirth.'

'But with money surely all of this can be altered,' Gemma pointed out. 'More hospitals built, more medical care, more schools.'

'More schools so more diseases can spread,' he muttered, and heard the bitterness in his voice. 'Physically things can be fixed in time,' he admitted, 'but the values of my people from the early tribal days have been sharing and caring—looking after each other. I want to find a way to keep these values while at the same time bringing my country into the twenty-first century.'

Now the woman smiled at him, and her smile caused more disturbance than her frown.

'I think I can see why your oldest brother chose you, not the one above you to be the highness,' she said, and he realised she was teasing him—gently, but still teasing.

'You keep mentioning the highness word, but that is all it is, a word.'

'A word with power,' she said, still smiling slightly. 'So, what about your profession? Will you still have time to practise? What hospital facilities do you have? And universities? Do you train your own doctors?'

She sounded genuinely interested so he set aside his strange reaction to the teasing to respond.

'We have a beautiful new hospital with accommodation for staff beside it, and a university that is still in its infancy, although our first locally trained doctors will graduate this year.'

'Men and women?'

'Of course, although it is harder to persuade women to continue their studies to university. That is one of the tasks ahead of me, the—I suppose you would say emancipation of the women of my country, so women can find a place and are represented in all areas of life. This is very difficult when traditionally business and professions were considered the domain of men.'

'In the Western world as well,' Gemma assured him. 'We just got started on the emancipation thing a little earlier than some other places. But you talk of your country—' Gemma sliced tomatoes and cucumber as she spoke '—and I don't even know its name. Is it an African country that you were working there?'

She glanced up at him and saw his face change—well, not change so much but relax just slightly as if an image of his country or one small part of it had flashed across his mind.

'Not in Africa but on the Gulf—a country called Fajabal.' He spoke softly, yet so confidently Gemma wondered if she should have heard of it. She ran the names of Gulf countries she did know through her head but no Fajabal came up.

'Fajabal?' she repeated, thinking how musical the name was.

'It is a contraction of two words, *fajr*, meaning dawn, and *jabal*, meaning mountain,' his deep voice continued.

'Dawn mountain,' she said, feeling again the familiar tug of distant lands—lands she'd never see except in pictures. But it was better to be thinking about the lands she'd never see than the way this man, sitting so close, was affecting her.

'Mountains of dawn is how we think of it,' he corrected, offering her a smile that confirmed all her feelings of apprehension. The man was downright dangerous.

'That's a beautiful name—poetic and evocative.'

'It is a beautiful country, small, but varied in its geography as we have the red-gold desert sands, craggy black mountains and the clear turquoise sea.'

Gemma finished the sandwiches. Maybe one day she'd get over her fear of flying and actually go somewhere like Fajabal. Though maybe not to Fajabal if all the men were as dangerously attractive as this one.

She put the sandwiches on plates, found some paper napkins and pushed a plate towards her guest.

'You are going to sit down?' he said, and knowing if she remained standing in the kitchen while she ate it would look peculiar, she walked around the bench, grabbed the stool beside the one Yusef was using, and returned with it to the kitchen.

'Easier to talk if we're facing each other,' she muttered by way of explanation, while, in fact, she knew it would be easier for her to eat not sitting next to him where bits of his body might accidentally brush against hers, and cause more of the uneasiness it had been generating since his arrival.

'I am pleased, no, more than pleased, totally impressed by the centre and by the work you and your staff do there,' he began, then he took a bite of his sandwich and chewed on it, leaving Gemma with the distinct impression there was a 'but' hanging silently on the end of the sentence.

'I will definitely increase my contribution to it, and I would like to fund your second house, but I wish for something in return.'

Ha, here comes the but. But how big a but could it be? What strings could he possibly want to attach that they couldn't accommodate?

Gemma chewed her own sandwich and waited.

Dark eyes studied her intently and he put down his sandwich, wiped his hands then said quietly, 'I want you to come to Fajabal.'

CHAPTER THREE

GEMMA stared at the once again impassive face, disbelief making thought impossible. She'd half suspected, from the time she'd heard from his secretary that the Mystery Benefactor wanted this meeting, that he might want something more than to check out the centre. But never in her wildest dreams could she have imagined this.

'You want me to come to Fajabal?' she said, thinking maybe her ears were playing up and he hadn't said that at all.

'You could leave tomorrow and both centres would keep running smoothly, you said so,' he reminded her. 'In fact, you have leave due and a replacement starting tomorrow.'

'How do you know that?' She snapped the demand at him but it was better to be thinking about his seeming omniscience than thinking about a place called Fajabal, red desert sands and all.

'Should I not read the reports you so dutifully send? Would you not expect that of me?' The words were cool and crisp and he seemed to sit a little taller—every inch the sheikh highness for all he was sitting at her small breakfast bar, eating a salad sandwich.

Gemma was reminded of her grandfather and had to fight the instant reactive cringe.

And fight back!

'I would have thought you had minions who did that for you—draw your bath, read your reports. You probably even have someone who could have checked out the centre for you, rather than having to come yourself.'

'Ah, but I came for you,' he replied, the dark eyes fixing on hers so it seemed like some other kind of message—one that sent fire racing through her veins and what could only be desire pooling in her belly.

Could he turn on that kind of magnetic attraction? Had he done it to divert her anger, however feeble it had been?

Impossible! She was reading things that weren't there into his words.

'So, Fajabal?' The deep voice lingered on the name, turning it into musical notes.

Longing replaced desire—if that's what it had been—a longing so deep and strong she doubted she could fight it. To go to Fajabal? To actually travel to a foreign land? To a land with the magical, mystical name of Mountains of the Dawn?

If only…

'Perhaps if I tell you of my plan you will understand,' Yusef said. He'd watched so many expressions flash across his companion's face he had no idea how to sort them out. There'd been wonder, and excitement, certainly, but fear, he thought, as well. Was she less confident than she appeared, this woman who had achieved so much?

She nodded in response but seemed to have retreated from him, something that caused a momentary pang, for he felt their emergency work as colleagues had forged the beginnings of a bond between them. While the attraction—but it was better not to consider that, although it was definitely there, as strong as he had ever felt for any woman.

'I spoke of education for the women of my country, and while many women have been attending schools and colleges and even universities for many years, there are women who are still outside the mainstream of modernisation. These are tribal women, from the nomadic tribes who have roamed all the desert lands of the Middle East right through the centuries, but in recent times more and more of these tribes have made their homes in Fajabal, escaping war and oppression in other countries.'

'People like those I spoke of, but instead of washing up on your shores, they have come across the deserts to your land,' she said, smiling at him so his determination to ignore the attraction weakened once again.

But he'd caught her attention—now all he had to do was keep it.

'You are right. However, settling into life in one place is not easy for these people and unless I can make it work, tribal divisions I have seen in other countries could arise, tribal divisions that lead to the horrors of civil war. If I can help these new settlers feel at home, all will be well, but right now, with overcrowded facilities, with children picking up contagious diseases at school, things are not good.'

'Could it really be as bad as civil war?' she asked, looking so anxious he hurried to allay her concern.

'I sincerely hope not but there are divisions already within my country—there are those who believe money solves everything, but these people, my brother amongst them, do not see the sick children in hospital, the malnourished babies, the overcrowded facilities. Until these issues are addressed, Fajabal will never be the great country that it could be.'

He paused and shook his head, trying not to think of his brother and the unrest that was probably spreading in his, Yusef's, absence.

'But surely this is a problem—the lack of facilities, the overcrowding—someone local could solve. Why are you talking to me?'

He studied her, trying to find a reply that would swing her decision his way, when her voice told him all too plainly that she didn't want the job. Yet now he'd met her and seen her in action with two very different patients, he knew he had to have her. As an employee, of course, no matter that his body had reacted to that thought.

'You looked at some issues in your city—women's issues and medical issues—and worked out a solution to meet the needs of two very disparate groups. I need someone from outside to take a look at what is happening in Fajabal. You have experience in helping women settle in a new country. The people, women in particular, I wish to help are also settling into a very different world—a modern world. It is not your actual training I require but your fresh eyes.'

'But surely there are a hundred doctors who could do that for you?'

She sounded desperate now, although he couldn't understand why she would have such an aversion to the idea that she wouldn't even discuss being part of it.

'*More* than a hundred, I am sure, but I fear they would fail because there is a philosophical aspect to it as well. I have already told you that I would hate my people to lose the values by which they'd lived for centuries. These are the things that have made us strong in the past and will again in the future. We cannot throw them away. You would understand that and could plan to help the new settlers with the courtesy and tact they deserve— helping them within the parameters of their lifestyles. More than that, you have the ability to instil your beliefs into others who will carry on the work. That is what I want from you.'

He studied her, trying to work out what was wrong. That something was wrong he had no doubt. She'd retreated from him.

'Is it personal, that you do not wish to travel at this time?' he asked, and caught a rueful smile tilting up one corner of her lips as she shook her head.

Not personal, then what? Why?

How stupid was this? Gemma chided herself as she pushed away her half-eaten sandwich. Although she hadn't admitted it even to herself, she'd been beginning to feel she was ready for a new challenge. Much as she loved the work she was doing, now both houses were established and running well, her life lacked the fizz and excitement that had accompanied setting up the centres and, to be honest, now they had this man pouring money into the place, she no longer even had the challenge of worming it out of government agencies.

And to work in a foreign country—helping women and children who really needed help, and teaching them to adapt to a different lifestyle yet in a way that was in keeping with their traditions, even to learn of their traditions and learn from them? Wasn't that the dream of a lifetime?

Of course it was—she could feel the excitement of the project humming in her blood.

Yet here she was, refusing to contemplate it because it entailed a plane trip.

She glanced at the man across the breakfast bar, hoping he hadn't noticed the shudder that went through her at the thought, because no way could she admit her fears to such a confident man.

'Are you thinking deeply—considering the idea—or wondering how you can politely say no?'

'There's no polite way to say no,' Gemma began, but he silenced her with a raised hand.

'Then don't say it. Think about it. I will have someone drop off information about Fajabal and an outline of how I see the clinic working, plus a job description and wage package for you. Maybe you would have time to study it this afternoon, then have dinner with me tonight to discuss it further.'

What could she say? The man had done so much for the centre, it would be churlish to refuse without even looking at his plans.

She nodded, and he stood up, pushing away his empty sandwich plate.

'Good,' he said, sounding as satisfied as if she'd already agreed to go to Fajabal with him, then he smiled at her. 'Remember, as you read the information, that we have already established a—is rapport the word I need?'

'You probably speak better English than I do,' Gemma muttered at him, unwilling to admit even something as nebulous as 'rapport' existed between them, although something certainly did. Unless it was all on her side—

'Not better,' he assured her, 'but I have read a lot of the English poets, even Shakespeare who is very good—very wise—about human relationships.'

Gemma found herself frowning at him, having only ever considered Shakespeare as a necessary evil to be got through in high school.

'You rule a country and have time to read Shakespeare?'

He smiled and she wished she'd dropped the conversation back at 'rapport'. His smile made her stomach, nearly empty, churn uncomfortably and she could feel blood heating her face.

'There is always time for poetry, as there is always time to hold a baby in your arms and feel the blessing it bestows.

Poetry can teach us much. One of our great Arabic poets once said something to the effect that love doesn't come from long companionship, but is the offspring of affinity, created in a moment. I am not saying that there is love between us, but was not affinity created early on?'

Gemma stared at him, hoping the tumult inside her wasn't evident on the outside. Surely he didn't mean the attraction she was feeling was mutual. Surely he was talking of their colleague-type affinity.

Yet the truth was there, deep inside her, that she did feel an affinity for this man—or maybe she was confusing affinity with attraction. Attraction was different, it was chemical, it could be ignored.

With difficulty, she decided as she followed him to the door, mesmerised by the wide shoulders and the way the broad back sloped down to a narrow waist and hips. He was a sheikh, a highness—he was so far out of her league it was impossible so it was time she stopped checking out his attributes at every opportunity.

Like now, when he'd turned at the doorway and smiled, white teeth gleaming behind those sensuous lips, eyes glinting humorously at her as he said, 'Is it safe to walk downstairs, or will some other wandering soul be waiting to accost you?'

Gemma stopped in her tracks, held frozen by the effect of that smile—that glint.

Oh, come on! she told herself. Get your brain into gear. You're not some thirteen-year-old meeting a heart-throb popstar.

But she could only stare at him, so when he took her hand and lifted it to brush his lips across her fingers, she didn't snatch it back or slap his face or do anything at all but continue to stare at him.

'Later,' he said, then he strode off down the stairs, collected his jacket and tie and, slinging them over his shoulder, departed. As he opened the door Gemma noticed that the limo that had driven him up earlier was still waiting outside, which was a funny thing to be thinking of when her brain was numb and her fingers trembling from a kiss.

Entering the foyer of the Nautilus that evening, Gemma felt an unfamiliar dread settle on her shoulders. Nothing to do with the man she was to meet—more to do with the fact that the posh hotel was the kind of place her grandfather had always taken her to celebrate a birthday or good results on a school report card. She had dreaded the outings, alone with her grandfather, certain she'd drop her knife or burp and bring that look of condemnation into his eyes…

She glanced down at her clothes, automatically, checking herself as she always had before a formal occasion with her grandfather. Her hair was as neat as she could get it, the wild curls pulled ruthlessly back and knotted at the nape of her neck. And even Grandfather could have found nothing to criticise in a plain black dress that skimmed her figure without clinging, black stockings and—well, Grandfather would certainly have criticised her shiny black pumps with their slender, four-inch heels.

But a woman had to have some weakness and, anyway, Grandfather was dead. He no longer controlled her life. But the reminders failed to lift her spirits and she looked around the new six star venue with more anxiety than appreciation. Although it *was* beautiful, the décor understated—big cream couches set on darker cream and gold marble tiles, marble topped tables between them; homely flowers like roses and carnations massed in crystal vases, and on the walls not the usual paintings but tapestries and carpets, ancient by the look

of them, the muted colours giving the big, airy space a sense
of continuity as well as welcome.

She tried to relax, but as she approached the desk to ask for
the sheikh, her discomfort from her memories changed to discomfort over the meeting that lay ahead. She had read and re-
read all the information, feeling herself drawn more and more
deeply towards the country over which the man now ruled.
The pictures his secretary had included in the bundle had been
deliberately planted, she realised that, but as she'd looked at
the ruby red of the desert sands under a setting sun, and the
black, rocky islands standing out of the turquoise water of the
Gulf, she'd felt a physical longing to see this place and experience the life of the busy, narrow markets, and enter some of
the white-washed stone buildings, or huge black tents.

'Yes, Dr Murray, Sheikh Akeddi asked that you be taken
straight to his suite.'

Suite? Of course he'd have a suite. Gemma followed a
black-clad staff member to the elevator, watched as he put a
key into a special slot, and then rode with her to the top floor.

The staff member led her into a foyer nearly as grand as
the one downstairs, though on a smaller scale. He knocked on
a door opposite the elevator and waited until another black-
clad man—though this one was in a suit—opened it.

'Dr Murray,' the staff-person announced, then backed
towards the elevator and disappeared behind the closing door.

'Ah, Dr Murray,' the man greeted her, holding out his hand.
'I am James Wharton, the sheikh's secretary. He is momentarily
unavailable but asked me to take care of you. Come this way.'

He led Gemma into a seriously beautiful lounge room,
with deep couches the colour of the richest chocolate,
polished brass and silver pots and urns decorating marble-
topped cabinets, and more tapestries on the walls, while the

marble floors had intricately woven rugs thrown carelessly across them, creating an ambiance of Middle Eastern splendour in a very modern setting.

'You would like a drink. His Highness won't be long.'

'Highness again?' Gemma echoed faintly. 'Does he always use that title?'

James Wharton smiled.

'Very rarely, although his close staff are using it whenever possible in order to get him used to it. In the beginning he started and turned round every time someone said it—looking for his father.'

'Or so they say, when, in fact, I think they do it to annoy me,' a deep voice said, and Yusef Akkedi appeared, clad now in less formal slacks, but still in a white shirt with the sleeves rolled up, offering her a smile that confirmed all her feelings of apprehension. The man was downright dangerous. 'James has provided you with a drink?'

'We were just getting to that,' Gemma said quickly. Mountains of Dawn might sound like a heavenly place but there was a steely resolve to Yusef Akeddi that suggested his minions had better not let him down. She smiled at James. 'Lemon, lime and bitters, please,' she told him.

'You will sit inside or perhaps you would prefer the balcony?' Yusef said as James moved to a cabinet against a side wall and opened a door to reveal a well-stocked bar and small refrigerator.

'Inside is fine,' Gemma replied, still taking in the beauty of the furnishings into which her host fitted so well.

He waved a hand towards one of the chocolate-coloured couches and she sat, sinking into the softness of it then immediately wondering if she'd ever be able to get up again.

'They are a mistake and will be replaced tomorrow. Far too

soft,' Yusef said, and although Gemma was slightly put out that he'd read her mind so easily, she also wondered if all mistakes that occurred in his life would be replaced as summarily. Humans who erred?

'You have read the information?'

Although she knew that was why she was here, the question was so far from Gemma's thoughts she was glad James handed her the drink, giving her time to consider what she could or couldn't say.

And if she came up with a flat-out no, would the drink be lifted from her hand, her elbow taken and she be escorted out the door—business done and possibly funding withdrawn from the centre?

That had never been said, or even implied, yet it was a niggling consideration. There must be hundreds of thousands of organisations throughout the world as worthy and as needing of funds as the centres.

'It's very tempting,' she said, 'and the women's clinic that's already established at the hospital could become a more general centre—somewhere women could go for information and help as well as purely medical assistance.' She hesitated then voiced an idea she'd had as she'd read through the information a third and fourth time, excitement at the opportunity vying with her fear of flying. 'But I wondered if perhaps I couldn't help you from here in Australia? If I couldn't work out some future guidelines for running the centre?'

Yusef studied her. She had a soothing voice, this Gemma Murray, while her presence, in her elegant black dress that set off the vibrant hair, barely tamed in the severe style she seemed to favour, was relaxing. An image of the hair unbound, springing around her head like a vivid aura, flashed through his mind.

Was he thinking these things to stop considering why she seemed so against coming to his country?

'Do you honestly believe it would be the same? Can you tell me you would make plans for a facility without meeting the people who would use it?'

She didn't answer, sipping at her drink, a look of—could it be sadness?—on her face. Then the pale eyes slid to meet his.

'No, I couldn't do it,' she admitted. 'But to tell you the truth, I don't travel.'

Yusef knew he was frowning at her but he couldn't help it.

'But you are a nation of travellers,' he protested. 'Everywhere I go in the world I meet Australians. Intrepid travellers, most of them, always to be found helping out in crises, I have noticed that.'

His guest looked uncomfortable, shrugging her slim shoulders, the simple movement drawing his attention to the swell of her breast beneath the black dress.

'I just didn't get the bug,' she said, although the flush in her cheeks told him it was an evasion.

Why not just tell him the truth? Gemma railed at herself. Just tell you can't get on a plane!

But to admit such a ridiculous weakness to as strong a man as Yusef Akkedi appeared to be, was, impossible. *She just couldn't do it!*

'Then it is time for us to persuade you to change your mind,' he was saying smoothly when she dragged her mind from the coiling fear in her stomach that just thinking about a plane trip caused and tried to rejoin the conversation.

'Perhaps a sample of our food will help. You are ready for dinner?'

He clapped his hands and another black-clad staff person appeared, pushing a cart laden with silver dishes, the domed covers concealing the contents but not the tantalising aromas of spices she could not name but none the less found mouth-wateringly enticing.

'These are traditional dishes of my country,' Yusef told her, leading her to a highly polished teak table set in an alcove off the big room. 'I thought you might like to try them but if you would prefer some other cuisine, French, Italian, Australian, the kitchen will provide whatever you wish.'

As the man who'd wheeled in the trolley was now setting an array of dishes on the table, and Gemma was fascinated by the variety of them, she shook her head.

'I would love to try this food,' she said, moving closer so she could examine the different dishes. Thick meaty stews, vegetables bathed in what looked like yoghurt, golden piles of rice impregnated with raisins and pistachio nuts, platters of tiny meatballs, bowls of pulses like chickpeas mixed with green leaves like baby spinach, baskets of flat bread—such a variety of treats spread before her, Gemma wondered if she might have let out an involuntary moan of anticipatory delight.

The staff person pulled out a chair and although he'd clearly intended his boss to sit in it, Yusef took Gemma's elbow and guided her into his place, taking a chair—which he pulled out for himself—across the corner from her.

He then picked up a plate and served a selection of food onto it, keeping the small portions separate.

'That will give you a taste of what we have on offer, but you do not have to eat it all. Just try what you wish to try—you may like more of one thing and less of another.'

It was too intimate. The food looked and smelled delicious but to have this man serving her—to have him sitting so close—was so disconcerting that Gemma, who'd been sali-vating only moments earlier, now hesitated. For some reason, the memory of his lips brushing across her fingers returned, and heat burned in her body.

'It is spicy but none of it is very hot,' he assured her, hopefully mistaking her hesitation, not picking up on the very different heat. 'We have few dishes that would burn your mouth and bring tears to your eyes, and certainly none we would serve a guest on first acquaintance.'

She glanced at him and found those coal-dark eyes studying her intently. Watching for her reaction to the food? Of course he would be, so why did his regard unsettle her? Because she kept thinking of him as a man—and not just any man but one to whom she was attracted, and if there was one lesson she had learnt from her ex-fiancé, Paul, it was that attraction was dangerous, the kind of dangerous that led to disaster.

She lifted her fork and speared one of the tiny meatballs, finding to her surprise, when she bit into it, that it wasn't meat but a grain of some kind, so delicately flavoured she finished it and wished she had more of them.

'Delicious,' she said, pleased she could be honest about it, and without being asked, the staff person slipped a few more onto her plate.

She turned to thank him but he had moved back behind Yusef's chair and his attention was entirely on his master, who was now serving himself a plate of the meat stew, adding rice to one side and some of the vegetables as well. He then took up a piece of bread and deftly used it as a spoon to scoop food into his mouth.

'As with chopsticks when you eat Chinese food, you do not need to use them to get the flavour, but in our country we use bread as a utensil, bread or our fingers.'

He balled some rice with the long slim fingers of his right hand and held the walnut-sized offering towards her lips. An apprehension she had never felt before flared through Gemma's body yet she opened her mouth and took the offering, hiding the flutters she didn't understand behind a nod of thanks.

This was taking the intimacy she'd felt far too far, yet she was probably turning a quaint Fajabalian custom of feeding people into something more than it was. There was a servant standing behind Yusef's chair so how could it be anything other than customary?

'That's delicious,' she managed, hoping she sounded far more together than she felt, because the faintest of touches of his fingers on her lips still lingered. 'Tell me about the dishes.'

His eyes scanned her face again, disconcerting her with their open appraisal. She scooped some vegetables onto her fork and concentrated on eating.

Why had he fed her the rice? Yusef studied her, wondering why his normal instinctive behaviour with women—to remain slightly aloof, to distance himself—had deserted him. He did business with other women, it was the way of the West and his country needed to learn enough of their ways to progress. Now he had business to do with this woman, yet his impulse to feed her was nothing to do with business, and as her pearly pale lips had opened to the invitation of his fingers, business had been the last thing on his mind.

'This, for instance,' she said, raising her fork above her plate. She'd asked him something earlier, but it had slipped past him as he'd contemplated some shift inside his body that was as unwelcome as it was unusual.

Attraction!

'The name of the dish?' she prodded, probably deciding he'd been struck dumb.

Ah! So she wanted to talk food. He could do that. He

pointed out the different dishes, explaining not only how they were prepared but also the history of them.

'Mostly our meat dishes traditionally were camel or goat but these days lamb is a great favourite in our country. The pulses and grains are the staples in a desert land for they hold their nutritional value when they are dried, so can be kept for a long time.'

'I've seen photos of ancient grain stores.'

Ah—an opening this time.

'Then you *must* come to Fajabal with me and see the real things. We have many still standing from ancient times. The desert is unforgiving in many ways, but its preservative properties are incredible. They stand like this.'

He pulled his pen from his shirt pocket and drew quickly on the linen napkin, sketching the old beehive shape of the grains stores, before pushing it across to her.

'Of course, being on the Gulf, the tribes who called Fajabal home were fortunate for there was fish and seafood in abundance so the necessity for grain storage wasn't so acute.'

Behind him the servant spoke in the musical cadence of their language, and Yusef turned to thank him before explaining to his guest.

'Abed has reminded me that the grain stores were necessary as grain was used as a tribute payment to whatever marauding hordes happened to be occupying our lands at the time.'

Gemma nodded, her finger tracing the structure he had sketched on the napkin. You must come to see them, he'd said, and excitement had surged through her as she'd thought of the mystery of lands she'd never thought to see.

But how could she?

Dare she?

Of course not, and remember that this man was using his

charm—his attraction—to lure her to his country just as Paul had used attraction to lure her into marriage—or nearly into marriage.

Forget the past and keep up your end of the conversation.

'I must admit history was never my best subject but it seems to me there were always armies sweeping across the desert lands, Ghengis Khan, the Romans…'

Would he tell her more?

She found herself hoping he would, if only to keep her mind off her stupid fears, but the conversation returned to food, Yusef now describing the different desserts he could offer her once she'd had her fill of the meat and grain dishes.

'Are you bribing me with food?' she asked, trying to lighten an atmosphere, which was growing more tense by the minute, though maybe that was her imagination, and the man who was the centre's benefactor was feeling totally relaxed.

'Bribing you?'

His voice gave more away than his face, the words sounding slightly startled.

'To come to Fajabal.'

The slight smile she'd suspected she'd seen earlier reappeared, although this time it widened into something that transformed his rather sombre face into…

She couldn't describe it but her physical reaction to that smile was even more startling than the transformation.

He's charming you, she reminded herself, clamping down on the reaction, dousing it with common sense. And he'll have a reason, so be on your guard.

'But I don't have to bribe you,' he said, still smiling. 'Surely you must know what you can offer to my people? And understand the challenge that lies ahead of us in expanding the medical services? Would not the challenge be enough to overcome your dislike of travelling? Look, let me show you someone.'

He turned and spoke to the man behind him, who disappeared, reappearing seconds later with a laptop.

Yusef opened it, and a screensaver came to life, a picture of the most beautiful little girl Gemma had ever seen.

'This is Fajella,' he said, his voice husky with emotion. 'She has no mother because her mother died in childbirth.'

He looked up from the screen, directly at Gemma, his eyes burning with a passionate determination she had never seen before in anyone, yet she recognised it immediately as the determination she had felt herself when she'd set up the women's centre.

'Would you have this go on? Yes, we have hospitals where this woman could have been saved, but with new settlers coming all the time, the facilities are overstretched to help everyone, and this leads to a distrust of the medical system and reluctance on the part of the new settlers to use it. It is to save the lives of women like Fajella's mother that I want you to come with me, to work with me planning and establishing a better way to provide services for all the women of my country, the settled inhabitants and the tribal people. For me, the driving force is for the good of my country, but for you? Is not this motherless child enough of a reason for you to at least consider the position?'

He turned the image of the little girl back towards Gemma and she knew she couldn't let something as pathetic as a fear of flying prevent her at least trying to do something for women like Fajella's mother—and perhaps Fajella herself in the future.

She knew she would say yes.

CHAPTER FOUR

BEFORE she could put her decision into words, Abed had re-appeared with a laden dessert trolley and Yusef was pointing out the different dishes, repeating what he'd told her earlier about the preparation and ingredients. Dates figured largely, as did yoghurt made from goat's milk, but as Gemma tried a little of this and a spoonful of that, she realised how clever the desert people had been in combining the few ingredients they had into delicious dishes.

'There is a flavour running through some of them that I can't identify,' she said, pointing to a pale pink milky-looking pudding that was strongly flavoured by the mystery ingredient.

'It is rosewater,' Abed told her, inclining his body slightly in her direction as he spoke. 'We have many uses for it. Roses have been cultivated in our country for thousands of years.'

'That seems amazing, although I imagine there is so much to learn about your people it would take a lifetime.'

'Several lifetimes,' Abed told her, while Yusef peeled a peach from a platter of fruit, divided it into sections then offered one to her. Remembering the brush of his fingers on her lips, and her reaction to it, Gemma took it in her hand but the slippery quarter slid out of her fingers and landed on the bodice of her dress before she had a chance to catch it and return it to her plate.

Muttering an apology, Yusef snatched up a napkin and dabbed at the stain, his head bent close to hers, the napkin brushing at the material covering her breast.

Did her breathing falter at his closeness that he stopped what he was doing, turning his head and looking into her eyes, awareness Gemma had never felt before flaring between them? Well, she imagined it was flaring between them for it certainly felt too strong to be coming just from her.

Then he straightened up and it was as if the moment had never been.

'You must allow me to pay to have your garment cleaned,' he said. 'They will clean it here at the hotel almost instantly if you wish to wear a bathrobe while you wait.'

Take off my dress and sit around in this man's company in a bathrobe? Mindboggling to say the least, so why wasn't she saying something?

Because she was tempted?

Impossible!

'Nonsense,' she managed, echoing his earlier protest. 'It's nothing that won't come out in the wash. And in any case, I dropped the peach, not you.'

He didn't argue but something had shifted in the atmosphere in the room, though whether for better or worse Gemma couldn't tell.

What devil had prompted him to attempt to clean the mark? Yusef wondered. Prompted him to put his fingers near her breasts? This red-haired woman was already disturbing his customary control, making him think things he shouldn't think about an employee. So why make it more difficult by touching her?

She was washing her fingers in the finger-bowl Abed had offered her, now touching one fingertip to the rose petals floating on the top of it. The backs of her fingers too had a sprinkling of the golden freckles he'd first noticed on her face, and he was fascinated by the glow the gold lent to her skin.

Fascinated by her?

He hoped not. He was far too busy to be considering an affair and though he needed a wife—definitely needed a wife because he was determined Fajella would not grow up motherless as he had—he doubted this woman would fit the role of consort to a Bedouin prince. His father's wives were not submissive women but quiet, authoritative figures who ran the household from the shadows. Not women like this one who was all light and sunshine—a woman who would be visible in the deepest of shadows—shining…

And quite apart from that, given that his brother still had designs on the throne, encouraging development and foreign investment to build a power base among certain sections of the population, there was the very real risk that he, Yusef, marrying a foreigner would strengthen his brother's claims to be ruler.

He sighed to himself, concerned now, not about the attraction he couldn't pursue but for the future of his country and its people should his brother take the throne. The problems he already saw would worsen as the society split into haves and have-nots, the old values of sharing and caring lost for ever. The thought caused real physical pain deep within him, but he hoped he hid it as he asked, as calmly as possible, 'So, will you come?'

The moment had arrived, yet Gemma still hesitated. While the glories of Europe had seemed attractive in the past, she'd never felt the allure she felt now towards a desert land on a gulf—a land where roses scented the air and flavoured the food, a land called Mountains of the Dawn.

A motherless child called Fajella.

And though her heart all but stopped beating in her chest, she heard herself agreeing.

'I will come,' she said, and sensed the relief that flowed from the man, although it still bothered her that he seemed to think she was the only person suitable for the job he had in mind.

But when he spoke he was all business. Perhaps she'd imagined the relief.

'You are not a traveller so you will need a passport. I can see that it is done as swiftly as possible,' he said.

'Actually, I do have a passport,' she admitted, remembering her dread as she'd organised it, Paul insisting she accompany him to New Zealand for a combined honeymoon and conference, telling her that getting into a plane was the only way to rid herself of her fears.

In the end, she hadn't gone, buying the second house and losing Paul, but she had no regrets on that score.

'So, tomorrow we will make the final arrangements. You are sure?'

'I'm sure,' Gemma told him, squashing her fear and speaking honestly. 'Not only for the opportunity to be part of expanding services in your country but for the chance to learn from the women who live there.'

'Good,' Yusef said, 'but we have talked enough for one night and the rain has cleared. Come, you must see the view from the balcony.'

It wasn't exactly an order, so Gemma, who'd decided, back when she'd said goodbye to Paul, that she'd never take orders from a man again, stood up and walked with Yusef to where the glass panels had been slid back, opening the room to the balcony and the view beyond.

It was a view of the harbour she hadn't seen before, looking west over the opera house to the bridge. Ferries and other boats in the harbour scurried around like bright water beetles, wavering reflections of every colour spreading across the water. But though she looked and admired, hopefully making all the right noises, most of her awareness was centred on the small of her back where Yusef's hand rested.

Waves of heat radiated out from that small patch of skin, and tingling nerves sent messages she didn't want to acknowledge throughout her body.

'Beautiful, yes?' Yusef said, and she turned towards him, to find him looking at her, not the view.

A gust of wind caught a tendril of her hair, tugging it loose, and as she put up her hand to catch it and tuck it back behind her ear, he also moved, also reaching for it, so their fingers touched. Nerves afire, she snatched her hand away but not before the damage was done, her hair now ensnared by his watch.

'Keep still,' he ordered, an order she was only too pleased to obey as this closeness had stolen her breath, and she doubted she could have moved if she'd wanted to.

'There,' he said, and she looked into his face, so close she could see the fine lines that fanned out from his eyes and the crescent indentations left by smiles in his cheeks.

So close…

'Beautiful,' he murmured, his fingers still holding the tendril of freed hair. 'So beautiful.'

Then his lips met hers, a touch, nothing more, yet that touch fired such an aching need Gemma responded, her lips pressing against his, opening to the delving of his tongue, giving and taking in a moment of sheer madness, their bodies linked only by lips and his fingers on a tendril of her hair.

She pulled away, feeling him release her hair immediately.

The words 'How dare you?' sprang to her lips but she left them there, unsaid, for she, too, had dared.

'I would blame the moon but it is hidden this evening,' Yusef said, his deep voice coming to her from the edge of the balcony where he now leaned against the railing, his back to her.

And while she still struggled for something—anything—to say, he turned to face her.

'So I will offer nothing but an apology. It is not my habit to kiss strangers, even beautiful ones, but your hair, the colour of it, the softness, it possesses a magic that, for a moment, made me forget myself. You need not fear that it will happen again, Dr Murray.'

Dr Murray? That's putting me right back in my place, Gemma thought, and although she knew she should be pleased he had doused the fires he'd aroused so quickly and easily, she couldn't help but feel a twinge of disappointment in his promise that it would not happen again.

'I must go,' she told him, more angry with herself for that twinge than with him for the kiss. Attraction was attraction—kisses happened. Well, they didn't happen all that often for her these days, but she did know about such things!

'I will see you to your car. It is in the underground car park?'

Yusef stepped towards her, as wary as he'd be approaching a wild horse. He'd like to think he'd been bewitched that he'd behaved so irresponsibly, but hair, red or otherwise, didn't bewitch. And even were it possible, he was a man of science, he didn't believe such nonsense.

Yet it would have been easier to stop the desert sands from shifting in the wind than to stop himself from kissing her.

She had answered yes and moved into the apartment, and he followed, his eyes watching the way she moved, seeing the shape of her beneath the fairly shapeless dress she wore.

Desire stirred within him and he had to wonder if it was a big mistake, to take this woman to his country. Yes, he needed her vision and experience to sort out the problems in the overwhelmed medical facilities for women and children in his country so he could move on to other matters of importance, knowing his people, both settled and tribal, were getting the best possible care.

But now he knew the attraction was there, might he not be wiser to find someone else?

Abed was waiting by the door, obviously intending to take the visitor to her car, but Yusef waved him away, summoning the elevator himself, and ushering Gemma into it.

'James introduced himself as your secretary. Who is Abed?' she asked as they travelled downwards.

Was she making conversation to cover the awkwardness between them? Or was she sincerely interested?

He studied her for a moment, seeing the flush that still lingered in her cheeks.

'He is my brother,' he said, and as the green eyes revealed her surprise, he tried to explain. 'Not by blood, but by…propinquity? Is that the word I want? It is our custom for children of our family to have a shadow child, one who is nursed with him or her, like a twin though not related. We shared a wet-nurse, Abed and I, and we have grown up together, travelled together, studied together, though he has a master's degree in business rather than medicine.'

'You have an MBA stand behind your chair while you eat?' she asked, as the elevator reached the lower level of the car park.

She sounded so astounded Yusef had to smile.

'He could have sat with us had he wished, but he chose not to,' he explained, but obviously that didn't help for she was still looking at him with a puzzled frown.

Eventually she shook her head, and started to search in her handbag for her car keys. Once found, he took them from her, feeling again the burn of attraction as skin met skin. A thousand ancestors yelled at him to forget this woman—to find another who could do his bidding without causing him a moment's unease. But as she led him to where she'd parked her vehicle he knew they were already fated to be joined in the endeavour of fulfilling his dreams.

As for any other kind of joining, no matter how strong the attraction, he doubted they'd be lovers, for once back in Fajabal he would be busy with concerns of state, and the women of his family were already looking for a new wife for him, a task his lack of interest in the project had relegated to them.

'I will phone you tomorrow?' he said, as he held the car door open for her.

She looked up at him from the driver's seat, her eyes questioning him.

'To tell you of the arrangements for our departure,' he added.

Our departure? They would be travelling together? Given the kiss, Gemma didn't think this was a good idea.

Not that she could say so!

'You are in a hurry to leave?' Dread pooled in Gemma's stomach, although maybe it would be good if she didn't have too much time to think about the flight.

'I cannot be away too long. I came to do a job and now it is done. To have to wait is inconvenient.'

Gemma nodded her understanding, said goodnight and drove away, thinking not about what lay ahead of her but of a kiss. Why was she thinking about such a thing when he'd promised it would never happen again and even on such short acquaintance she was reasonably sure he was a man who kept his promises.

But the kiss had made her feel alive—really alive—for the first time since she'd started the centre, since she'd tackled charities and government agencies, bullying and pleading, shoring up her case with facts and figures about women who suffered and even died needlessly in childbirth, until she'd finally got the funding to begin to fulfil an idea that had become an obsession.

Did he even know the potency of his kisses?

Was that how he got his way when orders didn't work?

The windscreen wipers slashed against the rain that had been deluging Sydney for weeks, and, kiss or not, Gemma couldn't help but think rather longingly of a desert climate. What a welcome change it would be.

Was she really on a plane to Fajabal? And not any plane, but some kind of luxurious private jet, as big as some of the overseas airliners she'd seen at the airport but configured so she sat in armchair-like comfort.

The days between her decision and their departure had passed so swiftly she'd had no time to dwell on the flight itself, or her fears, and even as she'd boarded, excitement then amazement at the splendour of the cabin had pushed fear to the back of her mind.

But now she was buckled into her seat, and the floor beneath her feet vibrated with the roar of powerful engines. She knew there were no memories of that other fateful take-off, she'd been too young, barely two, yet the fear was there, and very, very real…

The engine noise grew louder and the plane moved forward, taxiing slowly at first then accelerating, engines whining their protest as they prepared to lift the huge aircraft off the ground.

Gemma closed her eyes and clung to the seat, feeling her

fingers sink through the leather, indenting it no doubt, right down to the metal or wood beneath the padding. But she couldn't close her ears to the noise which whirled in her head like terror incarnate, filling all the space in her brain with a terror too big to battle.

Would she faint? Pass out? Maybe that would be the best thing…

'You didn't tell me you had a fear of flying.'

A deep accusatory voice at her elbow, and a warm hand closed on her white-knuckled grip on the chair arm, but she couldn't open her eyes or release her hand. Images buried deep inside now flared across her mind and her heart raced erratically.

'Is there anything I can do?' the deep voice asked, caring now, not accusing at all.

Was there anything?

She didn't know. She'd only imagined this terror, never really felt it—not through and through so every cell in her body was filled with it, wound so tightly she wondered she hadn't already shattered into a million pieces.

'Perhaps a diversion,' the deep voice said, making very little sense. Unless he meant a physical diversion. He'd order the plane returned to land. She could breathe again!

But she couldn't breathe for his idea of a diversion *was* physical. Very physical! He was kissing her, his lips firm and hard against hers while his arm, hot and heavy, now snaked around her shoulders, holding her firmly, drawing her close, his mouth increasing the pressure on her lips.

Hands still clamped on the chair arms, Gemma felt the kiss steal into her blood, slowly but surely easing some of the tension in her body. His lips pressed more firmly, parting hers so his tongue could invade her mouth—an exciting invasion, or was her terror adding a new dimension to a kiss?

Gently but surely he coaxed a response, so now she was kissing him back, exploring his lips as he had explored hers, learning the taste of him, the tart tang of his aftershave, the trace of man beneath it. Now her heart raced for a different reason, especially as he manoeuvred so her hand, the one closest to him, gave up its grip on the chair and somehow came to rest behind his head.

Silky soft hair, cut short, but not so short her fingers couldn't find purchase in it. But now she needed to hold on for a different reason, now she needed to anchor herself to him as he awoke sensations within her that she had never felt before. His hand cupped her breast, his thumb teasing at her nipple, and through the cloth of shirt and bra she felt it harden to his touch-rasp and scratch against what she'd always thought was soft material.

Her body softened, opening to sensation, wanting more, needing more.

'We are airborne, now it will get easier.' He spoke against her lips, the words surprising her so much she gave a little gasp.

Did he read it as renewed fear that his arm tightened its hold on her shoulders, or that his mouth once again closed in with a kiss? She had no answer—couldn't answer now, too involved in kissing.

'And we can remove the arm of this chair so we can be more comfortable.'

Comfortable? Up here, thousands of feet above the earth, and he expected her to be comfortable?

Terror returned but he countered it again, renewing his attack on her lips, his free hand roaming her body, setting fire to it in places she'd never imagined as erotic—inside her forearm with a gentle stroking, the back of her neck with tiny flicks, his mouth following his fingers now, tongue licking, teeth nipping.

What was he doing? Yusef held the woman in his arms, feeling the fear still lingering in her tense muscles and quivering limbs. But kissing her had definitely made her forget the fear for the time it had taken for the plane to lift into the sky, so if he could kiss her until she relaxed and maybe slept, would not the journey be easier for her?

With one hand behind her head, holding it but also toying with the knot into which she'd wound her hair, he deepened the kiss.

If he answered honestly, it wasn't totally altruistic because he could not remember ever feeling so attracted to a woman—instantly attracted from the moment they'd first met, when she'd been worried and stressed over her patient and her wild hair had been escaping its confinement.

But for all that he'd given in to temptation and kissed her on the balcony, he definitely would have resisted the attraction had he not seen her terror on take-off and been willing to do anything to alleviate it. He hadn't needed Abed, who never missed much, to remind him that an affair between them would be impossible back in Fajabal, in the full glare of the public eye and with the weight of public opinion still divided about his succession.

Her mouth tasted of strawberries, with something astringent, maybe lemon juice, squeezed over them. It should have been offputting yet he found the sweet and sour enticing, tasting, and tasting again, his tongue delving deeper, his body hardening when she gave a little sigh of pleasure as if welcoming his invasion.

CHAPTER FIVE

'SIR, sir!'

The urgency in the words shocked him back to the present and he turned to find the flight engineer hovering by his side.

'It is Massa, the chief pilot, he has collapsed.'

Yusef's first thought was for the woman he'd been kissing.

'It is all right, we are quite safe. The plane has two pilots and I am also qualified to fly this aircraft,' he assured her, but she was no longer in his arms, or in her seat. She was on her feet and moving towards the front of the plane. Fear forgotten as she reacted automatically to an emergency? Could she be so strong?

'Wouldn't pilots have regular health checks?' she asked as he joined her, passing her, in fact, telling her he could handle it.

'Of course they do, but even the healthiest of people can have an unexpected heart attack or stroke,' he reminded her, as she ignored his assurances that she wasn't needed and followed him into the cockpit.

Massa was slumped forward over the controls, apparently not engaging any of them for the plane flew on steadily, the copilot doing his best to ignore his comatose colleague and concentrate on his job.

The cockpit looked just like those she'd seen in movies. Why this absurd thought should occur to Gemma as she watched Yusef and the man who'd summoned him lift the pilot from his seat she didn't know. She thrust the thought away to concentrate on emergency procedures. Stroke or heart attack, aspirin was good. The man was stirring, he could take it orally.

He was on the floor in the narrow entrance to the cockpit, groaning now, hand pressing his chest, talking to Yusef who was feeling for a pulse, checking his breathing, while the second man loosened the pilot's clothing.

'His pain says it's heart. We'll move him to the master suite,' Yusef said, and Gemma followed the two men and their burden, marvelling that they carried the heavy man so easily.

The master suite was another marvel! They pushed through a curtained partition, heavy dark blue velvet drapes opening to reveal a bedroom of such luxury it would shame the best of hotel suites.

Yusef was issuing orders, but in a language Gemma didn't understand. The staff people who had gathered, three of them now, rushed off to do his bidding.

'The plane is used to transport ill people from time to time so we have a good selection of medical equipment on board,' he explained to Gemma. 'We can give him oxygen, hook him up to an ECG monitor, relieve his pain and stabilise him.'

And even as he spoke staff members returned with equipment, including, Gemma was pleased to see, a defibrillator in case the man collapsed again.

'Will you turn back?' she asked, as Yusef fitted an oxygen mask to the patient's face and adjusted the flow.

'That depends on you,' he said, looking up so his dark eyes focussed on her face with a peculiar intensity.

She hid a tremor of reaction—this man did intensity far too well…

'On me?'

'On whether you are willing to watch him if we fly on to Fajabal. I know he would prefer to be hospitalised at home, close to his family and friends, and in a place where he understands the language, but I can't leave the copilot to do all the flying.'

He hesitated then smiled at her.

'I'm a good pilot,' he added, but it was the smile, not the reassurance, that decided Gemma. She knew instinctively that if they turned back now, she wouldn't go to Fajabal, wouldn't see the mountains of the dawn, wouldn't feel the heat of the desert sands or smell the perfume of the rose gardens.

Wouldn't see Yusef smile again…

'Of course I'll watch him,' she heard herself say as Yusef, one hundred per cent of his attention back on his patient, passed her the blood-pressure monitor then, assuming she would take over that task, went ahead and attached the ECG monitor leads to Massa's chest.

With Yusef on one side of the patient, getting close on the other side involved climbing up onto the big bed. Gemma managed it, but it was awkward—not unlike treating a patient on the floor, she reminded herself.

One of the staff handed Gemma a notebook and she jotted down the time and Massa's blood pressure, then checked his pulse and noted that as well. The ECG leads in place and the monitor set up, Yusef was now inserting a catheter into Massa's forearm to provide IV access.

'I'll use morphine rather than nitrates to relieve the pain in case the nitrates cause hypotension. The fewer complications the better.'

Gemma suspected Yusef was talking more to himself than

to her, especially when he rummaged through a case of drugs, muttering, 'Antiemetic, there must be an antiemetic here.'

Eventually he had all he wanted and had set up a drip, titrating the pain relief and antiemetic into the fluid that was entering Massa's vein. He took the notebook from Gemma, who was still perched on the far side of the bed, and wrote in the dosages and time, then frowned at her.

'Are you happy with this?'

He looked so concerned she had to smile.

'Not exactly happy to see a man in pain, but I'm confident I can take care of him while you fly the plane, if that's what you're asking.'

He nodded, accepting her reply.

'One of the staff will be with you at all times, so send for me if you need me. I don't need to be in the cockpit all the time so I will return to relieve you from time to time.'

He spoke stiffly, and she realised that it was difficult for such a confident, self-sufficient man to have to rely on someone else—or maybe not so much rely, because he had staff on whom he must rely, but to ask a favour of someone.

Especially a woman?

She didn't know him well enough to guess, so she assured him she'd take good care of Massa. Yet still Yusef hesitated, his eyes scanning her face as if trying to read something there.

'Go,' she said, disconcerted by his gaze, disconcerted because her own gaze snagged on his lips and she was remembering the effect they'd had on her—remembering the kiss…

The morphine had made Massa sleepy, so there was little for Gemma to do except check the monitor from time to time and make sure the fluid was flowing into a vein, not into subcutaneous tissue. Movement could sometimes dislodge the catheter, but Massa's arm showed no sign of the tell-tale swelling.

Gemma looked around the suite, marvelling that such a luxurious bedroom could exist on an aircraft.

Aircraft!

She was still on a plane!

The panic threatened to return but she held it back, fussing over Massa, removing his shoes and socks, then his trousers so he was lying in his underwear on the bed. Now she could cover him. She moved around the bed as easily as she would in the centre back at home, and although it had been years since she'd dealt with a heart-attack patient, her training reasserted itself and she took regular readings of his pulse and blood pressure, jotting them down in the notebook, checking the figures against the previous ones to reassure herself he was more comfortable now than he had been when they had first moved him.

The problem was furniture, or the lack of it. Obviously, being on a plane, all furniture had to be fixed so there were no chairs she could pull over beside the bed to sit on. The staff member Yusef had left with her had solved the problem by sitting on the floor on the far side of the big room, but if she sat on the floor she couldn't see Massa on the bed.

The only solution was to perch on the bed itself—it was certainly big enough for the patient and any number of caregivers, but not particularly comfortable to be sitting without a back-rest.

'The plane is on autopilot and the copilot is over the shock of Massa's collapse and happy to be in charge so I can sit with him while you rest.'

Yusef had entered quietly so his voice startled Gemma, who was reading the printout from the ECG monitor, tracing the waves that also showed Massa's heart had returned to a normal rhythm.

'I don't need to rest,' she replied. 'It's not as if I'm doing anything taxing. If anyone should rest, it's you.'

'I will rest when we are all safely home,' he said, looking down at Massa then walking around the big bed to sit on the edge of it, right beside Gemma. He picked up the notebook and read through her notes.

'He is well so we are left with you,' Yusef said, and Gemma, already disconcerted by his closeness, turned to frown at him.

'Me?'

'Your fear of flying. You will tell me?'

A question yet at the same time a command, and whether it was because he was a virtual stranger, or because of the bizarre circumstances in which she found herself, all at once Gemma felt she *could* talk about that far-off time.

So she did, spilling out the story of her father's delight in flying, of his pride in his small plane, repeating the stories Grandfather's housekeeper had told her, the housekeeper reluctant but persuaded by a persistent small girl.

'My grandfather had forbidden her to talk to me about my parents and in particular of the accident that had killed them both, but I had to find out some time.'

'Was he protecting you?' Yusef asked, and Gemma smiled, although she knew there was no humour in her expression.

'I'd like to think he thought he was, for that would mean he cared, but I doubt that was his reasoning. He was a man who believed one should never look back. One went on regardless of the past—stoic and uncomplaining—although it's a little hard for a two-year-old to be stoic.'

'You were two years old?' Yusef queried, and his arms went around her, clasping her against his body as if to protect her from the hurt of her childhood.

She nodded against his chest.

'I really don't remember anything about the actual crash.

All I know is that it took a day for someone to find the wreckage and me inside it, and because I don't remember it's ridiculous I should be so terrified of flying.'

'Ridiculous?' Yusef echoed, his voice rasping out the word as her story had elicited such emotion in him his throat was tight. 'You're a doctor, you know there would be memories. Some psychiatrists even claim we can remember being in the womb, but at two there would have been memories. Yet you let yourself be persuaded to come to Fajabal, knowing you'd have to put yourself through such torture?'

'I had to get over it some time,' she muttered. 'And the challenge of what you hope to accomplish in Fajabal seemed so exciting.'

'Exciting enough to go through what you obviously went through on take-off?' He didn't know why he was persisting— surely not to convince himself that her response to his kiss had been more than fear-generated?

'Exciting enough for me to think maybe the fear was all in my mind, and maybe I would take to flying like a duck to water.'

He knew she hadn't for she'd shivered as she'd spoken, and he drew her close again, his hands comforting her now, although comfort was only a breath away from excitement.

Had she felt it too, that she pushed away, distancing herself, although distance was difficult when they were sharing half a bed.

'If you really want to sit with him, I could go back to my seat,' she said, and though the words were brave he saw the colour seep from her skin, leaving the scattering of golden freckles standing out like a rash. Was the thought of moving about on the plane so terrifying?

He could not imagine such fear.

'No, stay here, but prop yourself up on the bed so you are

comfortable,' he suggested, then he piled pillows against the bedhead to make a back-rest for her. 'I'm sure Massa won't mind sharing the bed with a beautiful woman, even if she is only nursing him.'

That made her smile and shake her head, denying his compliment, but the colour had returned to her face and she had relaxed again. Or relaxed as much as she could, given her terror. She moved onto the bed, resting against the pillows, and his body stirred to see her there. He had to get away—it was bad enough that kissing her had confirmed the attraction he felt towards her, but for his body to be seeing her on the bed and thinking—

'I will send someone in with something for you to eat, and check again on you both shortly.'

Practicality, that was the way to handle it!

Gemma watched him disappear through the blue curtains, and steadfastly denied that the hollow feeling in her belly could be loss. It was because the fear still lurked like dark shadows in the corners of her mind that she minded his departure. At least when he was close she could forget it. But now she considered the fear she realised it wasn't the nail-biting, hand-clenching terror it had been. Somehow it seemed stupid to be afraid of flying when she was sitting up on snowy white silk sheets in a huge, many-pillowed bed.

Beside a patient! she reminded herself, and turned her attention to Massa. He was sleeping now, his skin less sweaty than it had been earlier, his colour better. Gemma brushed a stray lock of hair from his forehead, wondering if he had a wife and children at home. Would Yusef have contacted them? Would they be worrying?

What would it be like to have someone to worry over her? She was berating herself for her foolish thoughts when the curtains moved again and, expecting a staff person, Gemma knew she smiled far too brightly when Yusef himself reappeared, bearing a tray which the staff member on the floor hurried to take from him.

Yusef spoke to him in his own language and the man departed, although it was obvious from his expression he disapproved of Yusef carrying trays of food.

'Not a job for a highness?' Gemma teased, to cover the delight her body felt at his return.

'Enough of the highness,' he growled, setting the tray down on the small table on her side of the bed.

Just as sandwiches formed the mainstay of hurriedly grabbed hospital meals, it seemed the little nibbly things on the tray served a similar purpose. The tiny grain balls Gemma had tasted at the hotel filled one dish, little pastries another, tiny tomatoes stuffed with cheese, a spread of small delights carefully prepared and presented to tempt the most demanding of appetites.

Yusef settled on the bed beside her, pointing out the different dishes, choosing from among them and offering them to her, one by one, so she ate like an obedient child, fear held at bay by his presence but a new fear building now—a fear of the excitement this sensuous enjoyment of food was firing in her body.

Who was she kidding?

It was Yusef's closeness firing the excitement. It was attraction, and attraction had let her down once before. Surely she wasn't going to fall for it again!

'You were worrying about Massa when I came in?' he asked as they both ate.

She shrugged, then answered him.

'I was wondering if there was someone worrying about

him at home,' she admitted, then because this was such a strange situation she found herself expanding on it. 'Actually, I was wondering what it would be like to have someone worrying about me.'

'You've never had such a person?

Disbelief radiated from the man.

'Not really, not someone who actually cared,' she said, defiant now because she didn't want to sound totally pathetic.

But she must have for he touched her cheek, a gentle forefinger tracing the lines smiles had carved beside her lips.

'So who brought you up?'

He asked the question as she lifted a glass of chilled pomegranate juice to her lips and the glass hovered in mid-air while she wondered whether she could avoid answering him.

He took the glass from her nerveless fingers and set it down on the table. Raised his eyebrows to silently repeat the question.

'My grandfather,' she said, hoping she'd conveyed by the coldness of her words that she didn't want to talk about it.

'You didn't love him?'

Gemma squeezed her eyes tightly closed, hoping to banish images of Grandfather as she always remembered him, a tall rangy man with a loud voice, forever coming up with new lists of rules she was expected to obey. Was it any wonder she'd fallen for the first man who had really showed an interest in her, who had listened to her, who had seemed kind?

She tucked the image of Paul away with that of Grandfather in the far recesses of her mind.

'To be fair to him,' she said quietly, 'it must have been appallingly difficult to be landed with a small child to bring up, and a girl at that. He could have just handed me over to his housekeeper, Mrs Rowan, and ignored me, and that might have worked out well, but he was big on duty was Grandfather, and he saw it as his duty to instil in me all the beliefs he held dear. He'd been in the army and ran the house like an army barracks but little girls forget they aren't allowed to run on the steps, or speak unless they're spoken to—little girls need love…'

There was so much sadness in her voice Yusef set aside the tray of food and took her in his arms again, holding her close and murmuring words he knew she wouldn't understand but hoping that the sound of them would soothe and comfort her.

When comfort turned to something stronger he couldn't say, desire rising in them both until Gemma pushed herself away.

'I don't need kisses out of pity,' she said, speaking more curtly than she'd intended because the kisses had aroused so much unwanted emotion in her.

He touched her face.

'I think you know it's more than pity. There is an attraction between us. You feel it too or you would not respond as you do. But…'

His voice trailed away although his fingers continued to caress her cheek, her chin, while his eyes looked deeply into hers.

'But it is impossible to pursue, my golden beauty, for all that I might long to go where it might lead. My country, as I have told you, is unsettled, there are divisions between the people. I cannot put it more at risk of upheaval by—'

'By having an affair with a foreigner?' Gemma asked, drawing back from him—feeling rebuffed, although she'd been telling herself to resist the attraction from the moment she'd met him, telling herself to resist it because she knew where attraction led!

Pain and disaster, that's where.

He didn't answer immediately, but when he did it shocked her.

'I was going to say, by marrying a foreigner,' he said, and she could only shake her head.

'You can't marry every woman to whom you are attracted,' she protested, and he gave a slight smile.

'I wasn't thinking marriage with all of them,' he said, then he brushed his lips across her once again.

'*Very* professional behaviour in the sickroom, I don't think!' she said, chiding him—and herself—and determined to get the conversation back onto solid ground. 'But now we've put attraction to bed as a conversation, what about your story? What was your childhood like?'

She'd moved, putting just enough distance between them on the bed for their bodies not to be touching, but Yusef was more aware of her than he'd ever been of any other woman. It had to be more than the magic colour of her hair and the golden freckles—there was more to attraction than physical attributes.

Which made him taking her to Fajabal nothing short of madness. There was enough tension in his country and enough unrest about his succession without him complicating matters with an attraction to a foreigner. As he had just told her, nothing could come of a relationship between them, no matter how strong the attraction.

'Your childhood?' she repeated and he realised that talking—about anything—was better than brooding over attraction.

'My mother left my father after I was born,' he began.

He caught the frown before she repeated, 'Left your father?'

'Of course,' Yusef replied. 'I realise outsiders have some strange ideas about our culture but divorce is possible in our land and actually far easier than it is in some other countries. My mother, for whatever reason, decided to leave—'

'Taking you with her, I hope?'

Yusef smiled at the vehemence in her voice and understood it. As a motherless child herself she'd be a passionate advocate for mothers.

'No, that was never an option. I was my father's son, but that was not really a problem because, as I told you before, I had a wet nurse and, growing up, well, our lives *are* different. Until I was eleven I grew up with all the other children—children of my father's other wives, adopted children and family children who just somehow come to live in the women's house. It is not a bad upbringing for young children. We were as carefree as puppies from different litters, tumbling over ourselves in play, hugged when hurt by whatever woman was closest at the time, a maid, an aunt, a grandmother.'

She was frowning slightly and he knew she was trying to picture a childhood so very different from her own, then she shrugged off her thoughts and smiled at him.

'And after you were eleven?'

'Ah—eleven—a big age in our customs. At eleven Abed and I joined my older brothers and their friends at school in far-off England, a strange, cold country with different rules and manners.'

He paused to return her smile.

'So, to a certain extent,' he said gently, 'I can relate to a small child arriving in a house run like an army barracks. My school was much the same—no hugs or soft words there. But we are talking, not eating. Try the little tomatoes, you will enjoy them. And when you have eaten, if you wish, you could have a shower.'

'A shower?'

'Or a bath,' he added, enjoying her disbelief but also pleased to have escaped the talk of his childhood. 'There's a spa bath just through that door.'

He pointed towards a door on the other side of the bedroom—right where Gemma had imagined the outside of the plane would be.

'A spa bath?'

'Great for relaxing on a tiring trip,' he said with the kind of smile that not only sent fire spinning along her nerves but also made her wonder about the uses to which the very big bed had been put on previous flights.

'I can imagine,' she muttered, although she kept telling herself that thoughts couldn't possibly make her jealous. And why should she be jealous anyway? There was nothing between them!

'Then you're imagining wrongly,' he said, and kissed her quickly on the lips. 'I've used this bed for nothing more than sleeping.'

Gemma moved away from him, edging closer to the pillows, disturbed he'd read her thoughts so easily, but more disturbed by her reaction to a kiss that had been little more than a brush of lips on lips.

'There are gowns in the cupboard over there if you wish to put one on after your bath,' Yusef was saying, as if their conversation hadn't been interrupted by a kiss. 'The blue ones are dyed with indigo, which in our land has almost mystic connotations of protection. Wearing one of them, you will come to no harm.'

Was it the certainty in his voice or the mesmeric eyes echoing the message that broke through the fear? Whichever it was, Gemma left the security of the big bed and without a qualm walked across the room to open the wardrobe.

'Wrong one,' he said, as she stared at the rack of pure white gowns hanging inside. 'Try the next door.'

And there was the blue gown—not one blue gown but two,

and gowns of purple, red and yellow, most of them decorated around the sleeves and hems with wide bands of gold and silver embroidery.

'You can, of course, choose another colour should you wish, but only the blue is dyed with indigo.'

Gemma pulled out one of the blue gowns and held it up, admiring the fineness of the material and the elaborate gold embroidery.

'It is far too pretty to be worn,' she told him. 'Maybe a princess could wear it, a—' she smiled at him '—highness!'

'It is an ordinary gown, the kind the women wear at home,' he assured her, although his voice was gruff, as if her teasing had affected him. 'When they go out, they will pull a black gown over it, but at home they are like a cloud of butterflies.'

Gemma heard the love in his voice, and remembered him talking of poetry. To describe the women this way, as he'd described the friends of his childhood as puppies, showed the poet in him, and for a moment she feared for him—this man with the soul of a poet trying to bring his country into the twenty-first century and at the same time ensure peace in his land.

'It's a job for a soldier rather than a poet,' she muttered, and when he raised his eyebrows she shook her head, unable to explain her thoughts without embarrassing them both, but more aware than ever of the link he called affinity between them. 'Perhaps I will have a shower and put on the robe.'

'You will find all you need in there,' he said. 'I will sit with Massa so take your time.'

She walked into the bathroom, reminding herself she could be in a hotel suite, admittedly on a very high floor, but, really, there was nothing at all to worry about.

There *was* a spa bath but Gemma felt taking advantage of

it was going too far, so she stripped off her clothes, turned on the water in the shower, then stepped beneath the warm cascade, using the bath gel placed ready for her on a hanging golden shelf. Shampoo and conditioner, four different soaps, aloe vera exfoliant, crisp new loofahs—such a range of bathing products filled the hanging shelves that Gemma could only marvel at them.

Soaping her body all over, she couldn't help but recall the magic of Yusef's hands as he'd touched her skin, and the kisses he had pressed, here on the inside her arm, there on the skin beneath her ear. Not that they had meant anything— those kisses. He'd been simply taking her mind off her terror, distracting her, doing her a favour.

Now a flush of shame swept over her, but she thrust it away and refused to let embarrassment spoil a wonderful memory.

Clean and fresh, she slipped into the robe, feeling the silk caress her skin. The deep blue colour made her eyes look greener, and as she pulled a hairbrush out of a clear Cellophane wrap she tried to see herself as Yusef saw her. But nothing in the mirror could convince her that his kisses, for all their heat, had been anything more than kindness, and she had to go forward into the new challenges that lay ahead without thoughts of the poet-king distracting her.

Easier said than done, for she came out of the bathroom, her hair twisted safely back into its usual knot, and the blue gown covering all her body, to see a flare of desire in Yusef's eyes, so unmistakable her body answered it.

'I will watch Massa now—you need to rest or check on your other pilot, and you probably have work to do as well.'

She'd tried to sound calm and businesslike, refusing to ac-knowledge the attraction she was fighting, and maybe it worked for the flare died and he rose off the bed.

'I will go but while Massa sleeps, you, too, should sleep. Rest at least.'

He touched her on the arm—where the gold embroidery crawled up the sleeve—and left the room, and Gemma sensed he'd drawn a line under whatever had gone between them before this. Now things will be different, that touch had said, and, understanding it, she felt a sense of loss.

You've got a patient, she reminded herself and she checked Massa's pulse and blood pressure, tore off a strip of readings from the monitor, checked them then put it all in the notebook. Showers on a plane, doctoring on a plane? Was this what she had feared?

Yet, for all the absurdity of this particular situation, she knew the fear was still there, hovering somewhere deep inside her, waiting to bite when she least expected it.

So, once satisfied Massa was stable, she settled against the pillows on the bed, closed her eyes and thought, foolishly, about kisses...

CHAPTER SIX

THOUGH kisses were the last things on her mind some hours later when, back in her own clothes, in her seat and with a death grip on the armrest, she suffered through the plane's descent. She knew Yusef was in the cockpit, and though this should make her feel safer, for he gave every impression of being an extremely capable man, it didn't seem to help at all. And without the distraction of watching over Massa, who was strapped to the bed in the big bedroom, Gemma's fear had returned with a vengeance.

She turned her attention to the window, and saw beneath her the turquoise waters of the Gulf and rocky mountains rising from red-gold desert sands.

The Mountains of Dawn? She'd have liked to ask Yusef it that's what they were, but even before he'd returned to the cockpit he had distanced himself. In fact, he had changed into his customary clothing an hour or so ago, appearing before her in a long white tunic like the ones that hung in the wardrobe. On his head had been a snowy white square of cloth, held in place by a braided black and gold circlet, so much the sheikh, the highness even, Gemma had felt in awe of him.

Not that she'd let him see it, simply offering a teasing bow, bending from her waist as she had been still perched on the bed.

'Do I call you Highness?' she'd asked, only half joking, but all the answer she'd got had been a quick scowl before he'd read through the notes she'd been making on Massa's condition and left again.

The plane slipped lower and lower until Gemma could see whitewashed buildings, glinting in the sunlight, squat, fat buildings lining the coast and further inland a cluster of cranes where modern edifices were rising, like the black mountains, out of the desert sands. Some were finished, high-rise business houses or hotels, but the tracery of the cranes suggested this was just the beginning of Westernisation for Yusef's country. She doubted he could stop it—he probably didn't want to— but she understood his dilemma, accepting the good that the West had to offer while retaining the basic beliefs and customs of his people—the values, as he called them.

A bump and they were down, racing now across the tarmac, the engines screaming as they went into reverse to slow the speed of the aircraft. Gemma eased her fingers off the seat of the chair, and undid her seat belt, anxious to check on Massa. Would the change in altitude have affected him? She doubted it, given the plane was pressurised, but anxiety had her heading back into the bedroom.

To her surprise he was awake, his eyes fastening on her as she came through the curtains.

'Am I home?' he asked, and she smiled and nodded.

'Safe and sound—well, perhaps not quite sound, but safe. I imagine an ambulance will meet the plane and you'll be transferred to hospital for all the proper tests to be done.'

She did a final check on him, then felt someone else enter the room. The reaction of her body told her it was Yusef.

'Well, you have now survived your first flight,' he said, as she turned to face him, trying not to stare at the imposing figure he made. 'I hope the next will not be as fearsome for you.'

The next would be her flight home, Gemma realised then banished the sudden spurt of sadness. Good grief, she hadn't really arrived, well, hadn't set foot on Fajabalian territory, and here she was getting maudlin over leaving!

Yusef was closer now, checking Massa as she had just done, talking to him in his own language, leaving Gemma to slip back to the cabin where she gathered up her hand luggage and prepared to disembark. She was hovering near her seat, her bags sitting on it, when Yusef reappeared.

'I am sorry I will not be able to accompany you on your first drive in my country,' he said. 'But I wish to travel with Massa in the helicopter that will transport him to hospital and I imagine you do not wish to undertake another flight so soon.'

He was teasing her, but Gemma felt a shiver of fear crawl up her spine.

'Definitely not,' she said.

'So, I have phoned a cousin who will take you to our compound and see you settled in. Almira speaks English and will look after you.'

It was a perfectly ordinary conversation and though Gemma thanked him for his kindness in thinking of her, she wondered what lay behind his words—what had caused the slight frown on his usually impassive face as he'd talked of the compound.

Was he thinking of their conversation in the bedroom when he'd told her of the impossibility of their attraction?

'So this is goodbye,' he said, and Gemma knew her suspicions were correct. He was telling her he would see little of her after this. This *was* goodbye!

Except that now he kissed her, moving closer and flipping one of the points of his headdress over his shoulder so he could fit his mouth to hers and tease her lips into a response so heated she could feel her knees trembling.

A *goodbye* kiss?

Surely not, when it was hotter than a promise...

Although it *had* to be...

Staff members were opening doors, letting in ambulance personnel, two men in white carrying a stretcher. Gemma stepped aside, allowing them by to do their job, watching as they carried Massa out, Yusef following, his attention fully focussed on his patient.

And although Gemma had already felt his withdrawal, and understood his first duty right now was to his pilot, she none the less felt a stab of pain in the region of her heart.

Foolishness, that's all it was! She prepared to leave the plane, a steward hovering over her, asking if he could carry her bag, her coat, then, when she thanked him and told him she'd manage, he ushered her towards the door, although once there he held an arm out to stop her proceeding.

Massa was being loaded into a helicopter not far from the plane, the lazy whap, whap, whap of its rotors filling the air with noise. The steward was holding her in shadow so she wouldn't be visible from outside and she wondered if perhaps it would be unseemly for people to realise their ruler had had a woman on the plane.

A foreign woman!

As the helicopter lifted into the air, the steward removed his arm and Gemma stepped out into the bright sunlight of Fajabal. She looked around her, deciding that all airports probably looked the same, but nevertheless feeling a surge of excitement at what lay ahead.

She'd barely reached the bottom of the steps when a black-clad figure, veiled so only bright brown eyes were visible, came tripping towards her, calling her name.

'Yusef has sent me to meet you,' the young woman said in beautiful English. 'I am Almira. You will call me that and I will call you Gemma, such a pretty name—it is all right with you? Or do you like Dr Murray? I could call you that.'

The young woman's voice bubbled with excitement as she led Gemma to a long black car, where the steward from the plane was already loading her suitcase. They settled into the big vehicle, Almira chattering on as the driver wove his way around the airport and onto what seemed like a main road.

'We will drive and I will tell you what we pass, and that way you will begin to get to know the way—you have a saying, don't you?'

'Get my bearings,' Gemma said, although Almira was talking again, pointing out the wharves where the trading boats came in from other Middle Eastern countries.

'We have been traders for ever,' she said, 'by land and sea. Our nomadic tribes were contracted to protect travellers and also carried precious cargo along the trade routes. Now we build big buildings to live in instead of tents, big buildings to do our business in. See, here is Yusef's new hospital, he is so proud of it and tomorrow when you are rested, he will take you there, for that is where your job will be, no?'

'I'm not exactly sure where my job will be, or exactly what it will be,' Gemma admitted.

'Oh, I know what it is,' Almira said. 'You are to help modernise the medical system for the women, the tribal women particularly, so things work better and the women feel confident using the services Yusef will provide. Yusef has seen many bad things in other places and senseless waste of life, children dying because they have not been immunised and women dying in childbirth—too often. This is what he wants to change, but too many people coming to our land too quickly have overstretched things.'

Gemma would have liked to ask more questions, but the scenery outside the car window was changing too much— from squat whitewashed buildings, some with camels seemingly parked outside, to newer settlements, walled compounds, and now high-rise apartment blocks and offices, their glass frontages gleaming in the sunlight.

A strange, slightly discordant noise broke the silence in the car and Almira reached into a hidden pocket in her black gown and pulled out a small mobile phone. She chatted away for some time, then folded it and tucked it away.

'That was Yusef. He wants you to know Massa is settled comfortably at the hospital. Now Yusef must go to work, he has much to catch up on after his absence. He says he will try to get back to see you this evening, otherwise you can talk about your job in the morning.'

Almira finished repeating the message then gave Gemma a quizzical look.

'You will miss him if you do not see him this evening?' she asked.

You will not blush, Gemma ordered her body, but she still felt heat rise in her cheeks.

'We have work issues to discuss,' she said, speaking coolly in the hope of squashing Almira's interest.

But the irrepressible young woman just laughed.

'Ah, work issues,' she repeated, then the smile slid from her face. 'But best it is just work issues,' she added, so quietly Gemma guessed she was speaking to herself, though of what, Gemma had no idea, unless it was to confirm what Yusef had already told her, that an affair with her would be destabilising for his country and his leadership of it.

She sighed, reminding herself she didn't want an affair with him but feeling the loss of something that had never happened.

The compound was just that, a high, plastered brick wall, with metal-embossed wooden gates set into it. The gates opened and the car drove through, past a courtyard that seemed filled with roses and around which maybe twelve huge houses were built.

'So many houses?' Gemma said. 'Does everyone have big families that they are so large?'

Almira shrugged her slim shoulders.

'Family!' she said, imbuing the word with affectionate despair. 'Someone builds a house and his brother then has to build one bigger. It goes on and on.'

The car pulled up outside one of the smaller houses.

'This is the guest house. The women's house is next door to this one. The servants from there will look after you.'

Almira led Gemma up onto a wide portico where they kicked off their sandals, then into the house, entering a wide vestibule with carpets flung across the marble floors, big sofas and cushions piled against the walls and more carpets decorating the walls. It should have looked strange, without tables or other furniture to break up the space but the colours were so vivid, the room looked welcoming. A young woman in a brown tunic and long, loose brown trousers appeared and Almira introduced her.

'I must go, but Miryam will look after you now. Miryam's English is excellent and she runs this house as well as other duties. She will show you where things are, get you anything you need, and take you to the women's house for breakfast in the morning.'

Then Almira, to Gemma's surprise, pressed a quick kiss on her cheek.

'Yusef has my number—call me if you need some company, or someone to talk to. I would like to be your friend,' she said, and whirled away as swiftly as she'd appeared.

'Through here is a bedroom and bathroom,' Miryam said, ushering Gemma along a passageway. But they had barely walked out of the big room than a commotion outside made them turn.

Gemma didn't understand what was being said, until someone spoke in English. 'The doctor, did the doctor come?'

'They talk of you, they need you—one of the children cannot breathe.'

Miryam translated, at the same time hurrying Gemma back towards the door. The women crowded around her, like the bright butterflies Yusef had described, their dresses green and blue and yellow, all chattering still, small hennaed hands waving agitatedly.

Inside the house next door an older woman was pulling a black gown over her coloured dress and it was she who moved to greet Gemma, taking her hand and talking in halting English, explaining the baby was ill, tugging her along, while grey-clad women Gemma took as servants followed.

Gemma heard the wheezing before she reached the child, and the moment she saw the little one's labouring chest and scarlet face, she knew it was croup—not deadly if treated as quickly as possible, but terrifying for the little girl.

'A bathroom—a small one if possible—with very hot water,' she said to Miryam, who had stayed by her side. The young servant led her directly to a room that held a shower and little else.

'For after the children swim,' she explained, but Gemma

didn't care why the room was there, turning the hot taps full on, taking the little wheezing girl in her arms, and holding her close to the running water where the steam was thickest.

'Everyone outside,' she said to Miryam, 'and tell them not to worry. She will be all right.'

'But you cannot hold her there, let her—her nanny do it.' The older woman who had taken charge earlier made the protest.

'I can't check on her from outside the door,' Gemma said, and waved the cluster of women away.

The tiny girl's breathing was already easier, but Gemma kept her there, talking quietly to her, although she guessed the little one wouldn't understand a word she said. Then the little arms snaked around Gemma's neck, clinging tightly, and a multitude of emotions nearly swept Gemma off her feet. Warmth and love and pain that the little arms were not those of her child, but after her experience with Paul, how could she ever trust a man again, trust a man enough to marry him?

The only man to whom she'd felt attraction since Paul was off limits—out of bounds—for all they'd shared a kiss or two. For all he'd talked about attraction she was fairly sure he'd kissed her out of pity—how humiliating when she thought about it. She held the baby closer, and whispered to her again, rocking her in her arms, singing a silly song that Mrs Rowan had sung when Gemma had been a toddler like this little mite.

The little one grew heavy in her arms and, with her breathing easy now, Gemma turned off the taps. She could only imagine how she must look, her clothing damp from the steam, her hair hanging in corkscrewing ringlets around her face. Wrapping a towel around the child to protect her from the cooler air outside the room, she opened the door, to find all the women still clustered there.

FREE BOOKS OFFER

To get you started, we'll send you
2 FREE books and a FREE gift

There's no catch, everything is **FREE**

Accepting your 2 **FREE** books and **FREE** mystery gift
places you under no obligation to buy anything.

Be part of the Mills & Boon® Book Club™ and receive your favourite
Series books up to 2 months before they are in the shops and delivered
straight to your door. Plus, enjoy a wide range of **EXCLUSIVE** benefits!

- Best new women's fiction – delivered right to
  your door with FREE P&P
- Avoid disappointment – get your books up to
  2 months before they are in the shops
- No contract – no obligation to buy

We hope that after receiving your free books you'll
want to remain a member. But the choice is yours.
So why not give us a go? You'll be glad you did!

Visit **millsandboon.co.uk** to stay up to date
with offers and to sign-up for our newsletter

2 **FREE** books
and a
FREE gift

Mrs/Miss/Ms/Mr _____ Initials _____   **M0CIA**

                                                BLOCK CAPITALS PLEASE

Surname _____

Address _____

_____

_____ Postcode _____

Email _____

MILLS & BOON®

The Mills & Boon® Book Club™ – Here's how it works:

Accepting your free books places you under no obligation to buy anything. You may keep the books and gift and return the despatch note marked "cancel". If we do not hear from you, about a month later we'll send you 3 brand new books including two 2-in-1 titles priced at £4.99* and a single title priced at £3.19*. That is the complete price – there is no extra charge for post and packaging. You may cancel at any time, otherwise we will send you 5 stories a month which you may purchase or return to us – the choice is yours.

*Terms and prices subject to change without notice.

MILLS & BOON®
Book Club

FREE BOOK OFFER
FREEPOST NAT 10298
RICHMOND
TW9 1BR

NO STAMP NEEDED!

NO STAMP
NECESSARY
IF POSTED IN
THE U.K. OR N.I.

If offer card is missing write to: The Mills & Boon® Book Club® , PO Box 676, Richmond, TW9 1WU

'I told you she'd be all right,' Gemma said to Miryam. 'They didn't have to wait.'

'We had to see,' the older woman said, while another young woman in dark grey tunic and trousers came forward, holding out her arms for the little girl.

But Gemma remembered how those arms had clung to her.

'She's asleep. I'll take her and put her into bed, then maybe stay with her in case it recurs although it shouldn't. Did the night suddenly become cooler? That will sometimes cause an attack.'

Miryam turned and spoke to the other women, who all seemed to answer at once.

'It was hot today,' she explained to Gemma, 'but in the evening the breeze from the desert came. It is cooler than the sea breeze at this time of the year.'

Gemma nodded, then after more talk among the women and several of them coming closer to check the little girl really was sleeping peacefully, they faded away, leaving Gemma with Miryam and the young servant.

'Anya is Fajella's nanny,' Miryam said. 'She will go with you and show you where the baby sleeps. Anya speaks English, although she is shy because she thinks she doesn't speak it well. His Highness wants Fajella growing up with both languages.'

'His Highness?' Gemma stopped herself adding, '*My* Highness' just in time, for he certainly wasn't in any way hers.

'Yes, Fajella is his child.'

Gemma was tempted to push the sleeping head away from her shoulder so she could take a good look at the child, but no doubt if Miryam said that's who she was, then this was indeed Fajella, the child on Yusef's screensaver. And her being Yusef's child might explain why *all* the women had been so concerned— although maybe they'd have been as concerned about any child.

But Yusef's child?

Why hadn't it occurred to her that it was his own child's picture? Gemma wondered as she followed Anya along passageways towards the back of the big house. And why should it bother her?

Although now she understood why Yusef was so determined to get a clinic set up in his country, having never known his mother and losing his wife in childbirth. But wouldn't his wife have had the very best of care? The toddler couldn't be more than two years old, and surely the hospital had already been built when she was born. Would none of the women use the hospital? Was that why Yusef wanted *her* here?

None of it made sense, and in spite of the sleep she'd had on the flight, Gemma was suddenly very, very tired. She followed Anya into a room furnished very like a Western child's nursery, with a cot and coloured wallpaper and a profusion of teddy bears and beautiful dolls. Anya let down the side of the cot but when Gemma went to put her charge down, the little arms clung again, and in the end, spying a mattress on the floor, where Anya no doubt slept, Gemma sank down onto it and told Anya that she would sleep there with Fajella.

'In case she has problems later in the night,' she added, so the young woman wouldn't suspect it was because Gemma was a softie and the clinging arms of the motherless child had tugged at her heartstrings.

It was late and Yusef was exhausted, but he'd heard of Fajella's sudden attack from his driver as he'd been driven back to the compound. Some woman with red hair had saved the baby's life, according to his driver, and although Yusef guessed Fajella's attack had been nothing more than croup, he was none the less sincerely grateful that Gemma had been there, and had acted so swiftly.

He walked quietly along the dimly lit corridor in the children's wing of the women's house, a path he trod every night when he was home, for he couldn't rest without seeing his little daughter, no matter how late the hour. He had not been here when she was born, and for that he carried guilt with him every day, for if he'd been here he would have insisted his wife go to hospital and her life might have been saved.

The door was ajar, and Anya was asleep on the floor outside the room. Yusef frowned at her and was about to wake her, for her orders were to sleep beside his daughter, when he heard a husky little snore, no more than a snuffle really, and realised someone else was in the room with Fajella.

Pushing open the door, the light fell on red hair and Yusef could only stare in disbelief, for there, on a mat on the floor, lay Gemma, her fiery red hair splayed across the pillow, the clothes she'd worn on the flight dishevelled and creased, but her arms were around his daughter, who was snuggled close into Gemma's body.

His instinct was to wake the visitor, to tell her this wasn't her place, yet why seeing her there should anger him when all he should be feeling was gratitude he didn't know.

Or did he? Wasn't it the stirring of his body, the shamefulness of such a reaction, that had angered him? He suspected it might be, but as he watched the sleeping woman, with his child in her arms, desire departed, replaced by a feeling he didn't recognise, a kind of churning deep inside him, a longing, but for what he didn't want to consider.

He knew it wasn't only the physical attraction that stirred him—he remembered seeing her on the plane, coming into the bedroom as she'd smoothed Massa's hair, frowning as she'd worried about someone worrying over him. It was this empathy she had for people—because she'd been so alone herself?—that made her special in a way he couldn't put into words.

Had his thoughts transmitted themselves to her that her pale eyes opened and she looked around, at first in puzzlement, then remembering, checking Fajella, before easing away from the sleeping child? Yusef knew he should say something—felt somehow ashamed that she should wake and see him watching her—so he stepped quietly into the room and squatted by the bed.

'I owe you much,' he said quietly, touching the backs of his fingers to his daughter's cheek. 'The women have told me what you did.'

Gemma moved awkwardly, trying to sit up, feeling foolish and vulnerable here on a thin mattress on the floor with Yusef so close beside her.

And quite apart from that, she must look a mess, totally crushed and dishevelled, hair everywhere. Yet now Yusef was touching *her* cheek, with the same gentle caress he'd used on his daughter, but his daughter hadn't felt heat spread through her body at that touch, or shivered, not with cold but with a weird kind of apprehensive excitement.

'I did nothing,' she finally managed to say. 'No more than anyone who'd had experience of croup would have done. I wondered, though, if maybe she has it often, if you've considered steroids if she does.'

Very sensible medical conversation for all that the words had sounded a little breathless even to her own ears, but the look in Yusef's eyes told her he was past conversations over croup and steroids—that he'd handle them some other time. The look in Yusef's eyes told her he was feeling as she did, feeling the inexplicable attraction that had flared between them from the beginning now stirring once more in his body. The attraction he said they must ignore!

'There are *so* many reasons why this can't happen,' he said, very quietly, then he leaned forward and once again kissed her on the lips.

Hard, hot, demanding! It was a kiss that denied his words yet at the same time confirmed them. Whatever this was that couldn't be still held them in a thrall, and as Gemma kissed him back, returning heat with heat, she realised that she would take whatever he could give her—that she would accept it couldn't be but still accept his kisses for of these she could make precious memories, weaving them together like a patchwork quilt so she could warm herself with them when she returned to her lonely apartment.

'You should go. I will stay with Fajella,' he said, when she pulled away from him, aware the kisses were so close to becoming more that pulling away was the only option. Now he was stroking her cheek, her neck, tangling his fingers in her hair, but she knew he hadn't slept at all on the flight and had responsibilities he needed a clear head to handle.

'No, you go,' she said, and pressed her own kiss on *his* lips. 'I am happy sleeping here, and the little one seems to have accepted me.'

'It is how I sleep in the desert,' he said quietly, touching the thin mattress on which she still sat.

Gemma heard the words, but heard sadness in them as well, and sensed the loss he had suffered, this man, when he'd taken on the responsibility of ruling his country. He was a man who had already lost so much, with his mother leaving him and his wife dying in childbirth. Was it his love for her that held him back from an affair with *her*, or was it really the fear of repercussions within his troubled land?

He kissed her once again then stood up, looked around the room as if seeing it for the first time, then departed, leaving his absence like a cold ghost in the room.

CHAPTER SEVEN

THE sleepy stirrings of the child woke Gemma, and she looked around her, totally bemused about where she was and why. A child's bedroom? A child in her arms?

The little girl was patting her face, and using a tiny forefinger to touch Gemma's freckles, smiling as she did so. Beyond her, standing by anxiously, was a young woman in a grey tunic and trousers.

Slowly memory returned, but not the name.

'I'm sorry,' Gemma said, speaking quietly so she didn't startle Fajella—*that* name she remembered as other memories returned. 'I've forgotten your name.'

'Anya!' The grey-clad girl dropped a little curtsey. 'And Miryam is outside. She thinks you will wish to bathe before breakfast.'

Gemma looked down at her crushed clothing and didn't need to sniff herself to know the assumption was correct. She hadn't showered since—no, she shut the memories of the flight to Fajabal resolutely away. Getting to her feet, Fajella in her arms, she gave the little girl a quick hug and a kiss on the cheek then handed her to Anya and slipped out the door.

Miryam led her back to the guest house, and waited while

Gemma showered and put on clean clothes, a long skirt and long-sleeved blouse, chosen for the trip out of respect for the customs of the country she was visiting.

'Should I cover my hair?' she asked Miryam, and was surprised when the other woman answered with a vehement, 'No!'

'It is all they talk about, the women and the servants and especially the children—the red hair of the woman who has come. Let them see it, although if you go to talk to women outside the compound, then maybe a scarf.'

'Well, I brought plenty of those,' Gemma said. She followed Miryam out of the house, retrieved her sandals and wondered who owned the rest of the collection set in a row outside the door, then followed her guide to the house next door, where sandals were again removed, only this time they joined an even larger pile outside the door.

The women were all seated, legs tucked neatly to one side and hidden by their skirts, on the carpets in the big room, and in front of them long runners of bright cloth held an array of dishes that reminded Gemma of the ones she'd eaten at the hotel in Sydney.

'Come, you will sit here,' the older woman who had spoken to her the previous evening decreed, and Gemma obeyed, taking her place beside the woman and awkwardly tucking her legs under her skirt. She would have found it easier cross-legged but was afraid she might be breaking some rule of etiquette.

The older woman introduced herself, then all the women around the carpet, but the names flowed over Gemma's head, the sights and sounds of that first breakfast in the women's house so bizarrely fascinating she could only look and listen.

Towards the end of the meal, children appeared, coming shyly into the room, greeting each adult in turn then relaxing, being children, pushing and shoving and laughing as they found places beside the women Gemma assumed were their mothers or grandmothers. To her surprise, Fajella made her way on still unsteady legs towards her, and although Gemma assumed she was heading towards the older woman, the little girl crept into her lap, only this time instead of fascination with Gemma's freckles, it was the red hair that held her interest, her hands touching it with wonder.

Fortunately, before Gemma could fall completely under the spell of those exploring hands, Miryam appeared.

'His Highness is here to take you to the hospital,' she said, a statement that for some reason caused a lot of chatter among the women.

Reluctantly, Gemma handed Fajella to the older woman, stood up, thanked the women for their hospitality and followed Miryam out of the room.

'They think he would have sent a car,' Miryam explained as they walked back to the guest house so Gemma could freshen up before leaving the compound. 'They think it must be because you saved Fajella's life he is honouring you by coming himself. They are most impressed.'

Honouring me? Gemma shook her head, knowing the only reason Yusef had come himself was because the project he wanted her to undertake was very important to him.

Wasn't it?

Of course it was! She knew that as soon as she saw him in the back of the long black vehicle, his head bent over a laptop, the points of his white head-scarf obscuring his face. The driver opened the door for Gemma and as she slid in, Yusef glanced her way and nodded, the gentle touches and hot kisses of the night before forgotten.

'I am sorry, I have emails to read and send. The driver will tell you places of interest as we pass.'

Ha! She'd guessed correctly. Hot kisses were definitely forgotten! Erased from memory…

Would that it was so easy, she thought as she looked dutifully to right and left, taking in the sights the driver pointed out but too aware of Yusef in the car beside her to process what she was seeing. Until they reached the hospital, a building she recognised from the previous day. The vehicle pulled up around the back of the building, and Yusef closed his laptop.

'You do not need to wear the scarf.'

The words were so unexpected—and so gruffly spoken—it took Gemma a moment to realise he was speaking to her.

'There are many Western women in Fajabal,' he continued, 'and many of our women who wear Western clothes, so you do not have to cover your hair.'

Gemma had to look at him now, but beneath the snowy headdress he wore with such casual poise his face was as expressionless as the blank glass façade of the building. His eyes were shadowed by the point of his headdress, but she doubted they'd have given much away.

Was he telling her out of politeness? Of course he would be—ridiculous to imagine he didn't like to see her hair covered, for all he'd run his fingers through it as he'd kissed her.

And you can put those memories right out of your head, she warned herself, before finally speaking directly to him.

'I don't mind, and if, as I hope, I'm going to meet some of the women who already use the clinic then perhaps it's appropriate I keep it on.'

'The nomadic women? They are not afraid of colour, or of showing their hair. For all that they are wary of Western medicine, they are more liberated in many ways than the women of my family. Wait until you meet them—you will see. But first I must show you the hospital.'

The driver had opened the door and he climbed out, and as someone else had opened the door on Gemma's side, she too left the vehicle and followed Yusef along a covered walkway and into the building.

'It is strange, coming here now,' he said, waiting for her just inside the door. 'Before, when I was here, I was just another surgeon, treated with as much or as little respect as I earned, but now, it is—not embarrassing but uncomfortable because although all the staff here know I'm still me, they treat me differently.'

And as they walked along a corridor to the left Gemma could see what he meant. Staff members they passed as they walked didn't exactly bow, but they nodded their heads and murmured a quiet, almost reverent greeting, not the usual cheerful hospital greetings colleagues shared.

'Here is where I believe we can expand our services to all the women of the country, and their children as well,' he announced, pausing at a closed door and looking directly at Gemma for the first time that morning. 'Until now they have been using the general hospital facilities, which are overcrowded and not specifically directed towards the needs of any particular group.'

Was it apprehension she could see in his eyes? Was he wondering if perhaps this whole scheme was nothing more than a wild pipe dream?

Yusef hesitated, uncertain now about what had seemed such a wonderful idea, then memories of Wardeh's death returned and he opened the door, seeing for himself for the first time the work that had been done in his absence.

Marvelling at it, as Gemma marvelled, her eyes wide with surprise as she looked around at the spaces that had been created, then out towards the courtyard where the mature roses he'd ordered to be planted were already in bloom.

'It's more like a palace than a medical centre,' she finally said, shaking her head as she walked around, touching a soft couch here, a wall tapestry there.

Yusef studied it again, wondering if he'd got it wrong.

'I wasn't trying for a palace but for the ambience of a tent, with the cushions and carpets and familiar, homely objects.'

Gemma had picked up a tall, shapely brass jug, gleaming in the rays the sun shed through the windows.

'Homely objects?' she echoed, the teasing note in her voice affecting him more deeply than her physical presence—and that was bad enough.

'It *is* a homely object—all families have such things—they are for oil.'

'Of course,' she said and his doubts doubled.

'You think I've got it wrong? You think I've overdone it?'

She shook her head and came towards him, pausing only a couple of feet away, looking into his face, his eyes.

'Yusef, I don't know if you're overdone it. How can I judge when I don't know the women whom you hope will use the centre? Or what you were hoping to achieve when you set it up?'

'I set it up as a special place for women who visit the hospital, whether for themselves or for their children, but the physical setting is the easy part-see. Through here, there are offices and consulting rooms and the usual hospital paraphernalia, but it is your expertise I need now to ensure I can provide a high-quality health service to my countrywomen.'

'Then I need to talk to the women who will use it,' Gemma told him, 'to find out their needs. Not necessarily specific needs at first, but general health issues.'

She thought for a moment, then said, 'For instance, with the new people settling in the towns, are there vaccination programmes for the children before they begin school? And are

the new settlers aware of these programmes? Do they understand the spread of childhood diseases and why they should
have their children immunised?'

She opened the door into the enclosed courtyard, letting
the perfume of the roses into the room. Turning to face
him, she asked, 'You've done all this—had it done—since
I said I'd come?'

Yusef frowned at the question—a strange one, surely.

'I couldn't do it earlier—you might not have come,' he explained.

'But someone would have,' she pointed out. 'You know a
better service is a necessity, so you'd have found someone.'

He nodded again, then came towards her, smiling as he remembered their meeting.

'But until I'd met you and seen the houses, seen the home-
liness you created so the women would be comfortable there,
I didn't know what was needed here.'

'And that was, what, five days ago? You've had all his
done in five days?'

Now he was really puzzled.

'Why not?' he asked, and she shook her head and laughed.

'Never mind,' she said. 'But I can't help thinking of the
couches at the hotel—they displeased you so had to be
removed immediately. You want a special room, and a rose
garden, and, *voilà*, it's there. It's like the genie in the bottle
granting wishes. I thought he was only in fairy stories.'

If she hadn't laughed he'd have been okay, but that carefree
sound echoing around the room, mingling with the scent of
roses, stirred his body and he reached out his hand to touch
her, draw her close, for all his determination to remain aloof.

He was going to kiss her. Gemma knew that as surely as
she knew her name. But she also knew it would be wrong—

wrong for her because these occasional kisses only made her longing for him worse, and very wrong for him.

She backed away, into the garden, reaching out to pluck a rose, nipping off the tender stem near the bloom.

'I need to meet some women, particularly some of the new settlers,' she reminded him. 'It is they who will not only determine the success of the service but will be able to talk to me of their needs.'

She paused, sniffing at the rose then looking up at him.

'It is you who said this cannot be,' she reminded him, raising the rose and touching it to his cheek.

His eyes darkened but his face remained unreadable. He studied her for a moment longer then turned away.

'The women,' he said as he walked towards the door, obviously expecting her to follow him. 'I will take you to the markets. It is there they would traditionally come when they were in Fajabal, and as most of them are merchants, they have stalls there, run by relatives of the nomads who have already settled here.'

He had to stay away from her! He could not afford to be tempted and sidetracked as he had that morning. Yusef cursed under his breath as he led the way back to the car. As if seeing her last night, with his daughter sleeping in her arms, hadn't been bad enough, but this morning—that first glimpse of her as she'd come out of the house, tendrils of her bright hair escaping from the dark green scarf, tiny freckles turning her skin golden in the sunlight. His heart had stopped, then raced, then plummeted.

Unseemly, that was the word. He knew it full well. It would be unseemly for him to have an affair with this woman, quite apart from the trouble it could cause in his already troubled land. But how could he avoid thinking about it when images of her kept flashing through his mind, images that sent his blood racing through his veins, pooling low down, hardening his body.

Sexual attraction! How easy it had been to satisfy when he'd been young and the juices had begun flowing in his body. A healthy and wealthy young man could find any number of willing bed partners and although he'd always been more discerning than some of his brothers and cousins, he'd had his share of what he hoped had been mutually satisfying affairs. Then marriage, Africa and Fajella. His life had changed, only to change even more dramatically when he'd taken the throne.

He sighed as he considered the troubles ahead of him. Yes, it might work, his idea of looking after the women, but it would take time and he doubted he had time, factions already being at work to appoint his older brother ruler. But he'd brought Gemma Murray here, so he owed her the courtesy of helping her find her feet not only in a new job but in a new country. He would take her to the markets, through the alleys to the women's souk, introduce her to some of the women then get Almira involved again. Almira could act as her guide.

This was opting out—he knew it—but given the attraction between them, and the impossibility of taking it further, it seemed the most sensible thing to do.

Sensible, he repeated to himself, and she climbed into the car beside him, setting nerve endings on alert at her closeness.

He opened his laptop again—pretending to be busy might distract his body.

'Too busy to point out the sights?' she asked quietly, and he closed the lid on the screen, which was still blank.

And looked at her—really looked—reading resignation in her eyes and a touch of sadness.

'I do understand—I really do,' she said softly. 'My grandfather's one weakness was old vinyl records and he used to play them in the evenings. There was a song on one of them that said something about it being the wrong time and the wrong place, and that's how it is for us, isn't it, Yusef? An attraction that's nothing more than an impossible dream!'

She reached across and touched his fingers very lightly, but far from dampening down the fires within him, they fanned the embers into flames, although he hoped he kept that particular reaction hidden.

'So, tell me where we're going.'

Her tone was bright—falsely bright, he suspected, but she was making an effort, so the least he could do was to follow her lead.

'We're going to the markets—the souks. Most of the nomad tribes are traders and have always had stalls in the markets. Some family members have lived here, running the stalls, while the others travelled.'

'But if these people have family members already settled in your country, wouldn't that make their settlement easier?'

He turned towards her and saw the slight frown that accompanied the words.

'You would think so, wouldn't you?'

Gemma had been doing really well, keeping things cool and businesslike between them, until she saw the wry smile twisting his lips as he spoke. It held sadness, but not defeat.

'So tell me,' she insisted.

'Families,' he replied, as if that explained everything.

'I didn't have one,' she reminded him.

'Perhaps that is a blessing,' he said, then shook his head. 'No, I don't mean that—families are the single most important and powerful unit of any civilisation, but they don't always have to agree. For instance, my brother and I disagree about the way our country should be run, and in the same way these tribal families have their own differences. The settled ones feel they established the stalls and have a right to them, while the new settlers believe, having supplied the goods for centuries, the outlets are part of their business and so, by rights, theirs.'

'Ah!' Gemma said, then, as several disparate facts slipped into place in her head, she added, 'And the business people among them would no doubt feel drawn to your businessman brother!'

Fortunately the car had stopped at the entrance to the market, and the conversation ceased. The driver opened Yusef's door, and he stepped out. Someone from the group hovering around a high-arched entryway in a white stone wall opened the car door on Gemma's side and a strange apprehension shivered along her nerves before she, too, braved the sunshine and climbed out of the vehicle.

'We have Western-style shopping complexes now, but many people, especially the older ones, still do all their shopping in the markets,' Yusef said, his voice that of a polite host explaining to a guest. Which is how it should be, Gemma told herself as he led her through the arch into an unbelievable wonderland.

The walls of the alley rose up on each side, dwellings maybe four or five storeys high, and on each side rows and rows of stalls, the first twenty metres mostly pots and pans—huge pots and pans—and metal jugs in beautiful shapes, and urns, and amphoras in silver and brass hanging from the walls and the spindly frames of the stalls, little separating each one from the next.

Then the spices, huge tubs of golden tumeric, the scent of cardamom and fenugreek, the mingling of a hundred different aromas transporting Gemma to a truly magical place.

Men cried out at her to buy their wares, holding up bundles

of dried herbs, but Yusef answered them, apparently joking with them for they laughed and waved the pair of them on their way.

'I should have brought a reel of cotton and tied one end of it at the entrance or dropped breadcrumbs to find my way back,' Gemma said as they twisted and turned through the maze.

Yusef turned to her.

'I will not lose you,' he said, and although she knew his words could have no deeper meaning than the obvious one, Gemma felt that shiver of connection feather up her spine again.

But before she could consider it—even to rebuff it—a new wonderland opened up in front of her. They had reached the silk markets—the women's place—and bolts of brilliantly coloured silk shone and shimmered all around her, dazzling the eyes and delighting the senses with the lush beauty of it.

Gemma paused by one stall, where a bolt of emerald-green silk, woven through with golden thread, all but yelled at her from amidst the riches. She ran her hand over the fabric, delighting in the sheen, the softness, then Yusef was behind her, speaking to the woman behind the stall, who was blushing and bowing at the same time.

A man appeared, small and dark, not bowing but nodding his head to acknowledge Yusef. Then he lifted the bolt of cloth and walked away, the woman talking again with much waving of hands and wide smiles, happiness radiating from her.

'What was that all about?' Gemma asked as they moved on.

'She was surprised to see me in the markets,' Yusef replied, but Gemma doubted that was all, for all along the narrow passage, messages were being passed and all the stall-holders were smiling at them now and chattering amongst themselves.

But the source of the gossip remained a mystery until Yusef stopped at another stall, this one selling intricately beaded headdresses and heavily beaded gowns.

'Ha! So the lion walks among the lambs and causes furore.' A tall woman with a striking face—dark eyes flashing against dark olive skin, a beak of a nose held proudly high—greeted Yusef with this teasing comment. 'The talk is all through the market—the king has come, not only come but spent some of his money. Now they say if it is good enough for him to shop here, people should forsake the big Western stores and return here.'

'You know I hope they will, Yanne. You know I've always hoped that. Not forsake the big stores entirely, but keep enough of the old ways to value the souks. It is important.'

The woman's lips parted to reveal a wide, white smile.

'I know you mean well, but will you succeed?' she said, and Gemma noticed the way Yusef, always so upright in his bearing, straightened even more.

'With the help of you and others, I will,' he said, no shadow of doubt in his voice. 'That is why I've come. This is Gemma Murray, Dr Gemma Murray, the woman I spoke of who will advise me on the establishment of a centre for women's and children's health. Gemma, this is Yanne, Fajella's aunt.'

Fajella's aunt?

Yusef's dead wife's sister?

Or some more obscure relationship?

It didn't matter. Gemma's hand was already extended towards Yanne.

'I was telling Yusef I need to talk to the women who will use the centre to find out what they need,' Gemma said. 'It seems there are already facilities but they are overstretched and not specifically for women so this makes the women reluctant to use them.'

Yanne studied Gemma for a moment, then she nodded.

'I will help you,' she said, and Gemma sensed that, beside

her, Yusef had relaxed, as if this was some huge hurdle he had overcome. Had Yanne sensed it also that she turned to him? 'You will leave Dr Murray with me. She and I will talk and we will meet some of the women. I will see she is safely returned to the compound at the end of the day.'

If Yusef was taken aback by this order, he didn't show it, simply turning to Gemma to ask, 'You are comfortable with this?'

'More than comfortable,' she said, then the ground rocked beneath her feet, noise assaulted her ears and the world turned blurry, billowing clouds of dust and smoke filling the air. Gemma felt Yusef's hand on her arm and heard him talking urgently to Yanne.

'Come,' she said. 'There's a back door. We must get out there, into the open.'

Now Yanne was pulling Gemma's other arm, but Gemma could smell fire now and pulled away.

'It was an explosion. People could be injured. I must go.'

Yusef had already disappeared and Gemma hadn't the slightest doubt that he'd headed for the danger zone—if danger zone there was. It would have been as instinctive for him as it was for her, and now she tried to push through the crowd of people trying to escape the narrow alley, going against the tide but with such determination she wormed and squirmed her way to the far end of the alley where flames were licking up the walls and the wailing of injured people told her she'd be needed.

Men were playing hoses on the flames, and in the distance Gemma could hear the wailing siren of a modern fire engine heading towards them, but a large crater at one side of the alley told her the explosion had been considerable, and remembering how packed the markets had been as she'd walked in, she could only imagine the number who might be injured.

Yusef, his headdress gone, his white gown knotted between his knees, was carrying a woman to an open space at the end of the alley. He scowled at Gemma when he saw her but didn't seem surprised, so she followed him to where other people were setting down the injured, more than twenty patients already lying there.

Gemma ran back into the alley and grabbed a bolt of cotton. The stall-holder, obviously understanding, passed her scissors. Water would relieve some of the pain of the burn victims but would dirty water cause more problems through infection?

She heard Yusef issuing orders and someone appeared with a big bottle of demineralised water. 'I will get more,' the stranger said, and dashed off again. Gemma cut and ripped the cloth, thinking to cover the worst of the burns. Once covered, she could damp down the cloth to cool the skin. All the patients needed fluid and she saw that some of the women gathered there were already offering water to the injured.

'Here, here,' someone called, and she moved towards the man, who was cradling a child in his lap. The little boy's leg was obviously broken, as if he'd been thrown into something with the blast, but he'd escaped burns. Gemma stabilised the leg with strips of cloth, then saw blood dripping onto the white material. The man, the father, had a wound in his arm and when Gemma looked she saw a shard of glass still sticking out of it.

It was deeply embedded and although the wound wasn't spurting, blood was pulsing out, probably because the glass itself was plugging the artery. Gemma cut more strips of cloth, wound two of them into a tight circlet and put it around the piece of glass then wrapped the lot and told the man to stay still.

Ambulances were arriving and she signalled to an attendant, showing him the man's arm, explaining the wound and the embedded glass, pleased the attendant could speak English. He took the man and the child in the first ambulance, along with the woman Yusef had carried from the fire.

Yusef? Where was he? Two fire-engines had arrived and men in uniform with fearsome-looking equipment were working in the devastated section of the alley where more injured people could be trapped.

Gemma suspected Yusef was also in that area, and though she feared for him, there was still work for her among the injured, the ambulances taking the most serious cases first, but leaving first-aid equipment for her to use.

She continued on, cleaning wounds, bandaging, warning people to watch for infection, although she knew that most of them didn't understand what she was saying. But they thanked her, and some shyly touched her hair, which as usual was escaping its confinement and springing up around her head, her scarf having been used as a sling long since.

'You should not be here!'

Yusef's words were so fierce Gemma shot up from where she'd been wiping the face of a little boy, and faced the angry man, his haughty bearing every inch that of a highness for all the filth of his clothing.

'Am I breaking some tradition?' she demanded. 'Is there a rule that says a woman can't help people in need? I've seen other women helping here.'

He glared at her.

'You know I don't mean that. I mean it is not your place— no, I don't mean that either—but you should have gone to safety with Yanne as I told you, not put yourself in danger coming down here, where more explosions could have occurred.'

'And you didn't put yourself in danger?' Gemma shot back

at him. 'At least I had the sense to stay out here in the open. You were poking around in there where whole buildings could have collapsed on top of you.'

She hadn't realised just how anxious she'd been about him until the angry accusation came tumbling out.

'It was my duty,' he said, very cold and formal. Putting her back in her place—a reprimand for yelling at his mightiness?

'As it was mine to help the injured,' she reminded him.

He hesitated then nodded towards the road where more ambulances were pulling up.

'There is plenty of help now for the injured,' he pointed out, his tone softer. 'I must stay while the fire experts investigate the cause. My driver will take you back to the compound.'

'But I need to talk to Yanne—' Gemma began, only to have her protest cut short by a touch of Yusef's hand on her arm.

'If you could see yourself you would not argue, and it is already mid-afternoon. You can talk to Yanne tomorrow.'

He waved his hand and the uniformed driver appeared, bowing to Gemma then indicating she follow him to the car.

But she couldn't leave, certain once she did so that Yusef would go back inside the unstable building. She looked into his dark eyes, past the smut and soot smeared across his face, and saw the weight of his responsibility there—and the pain of it.

He would do what he had to do—she knew that—and all she could say was, 'Be careful. Please!'

A slight movement of his lips, the gleam of white teeth behind those lips.

'I will,' he said, and walked away, back to where chaos still reigned as the stall-holders tried to salvage something from the ruins of their wares.

CHAPTER EIGHT

BACK in the guest house, Gemma thanked the driver and hurried into the building, not wanting anyone to see her in her filthy state. But it was as if Miryam was expecting her, coming to her and leading her into the bathroom where she'd run a bath, scattered rose-petals on the surface, and laid out one of the indigo gowns.

'It is comfortable for you to rest in,' she said to Gemma. 'You bathe and I will bring food and tea to your room so you can eat then sleep. The people are grateful for what you do today.'

'How could you know what's happened?' Gemma asked, then she saw herself in the bathroom mirror and laughed. 'Apart from the fact that I look such a mess!

Miryam shrugged.

'We hear things. Everyone hears things,' she said, and Gemma could only shake her head. Then she remembered the explosion and fear for Yusef gripped her again. Had someone known he was at the souk? Had the explosion been an attempt on his life? Was the unrest he spoke of more serious than she'd thought?

'If you hear things,' she said urgently to Miryam, 'do you know what happened to cause the explosion and fire?'

'Of course,' Miryam said. 'It was gas. One of the first things the new highness did was to tell people they must not use old gas tanks. He even made new ones available so people could come and take them for free but the traders in the markets they know best and keep using the old ones. It is because they explode the new highness wanted them changed, but never has there been a bang as big as that one, so maybe now the traders will learn.'

Gemma thanked Miryam, and shut the bathroom door, pondering the problems of the 'new highness' as she stripped and climbed into the lightly scented bath. From tribal unrest to matters as small as replacement gas tanks—did the man have to handle everything himself? Concern himself with even such minor things as gas tanks?

Of course he would if they were matters of life and death, she realised as she washed greasy soot and smears of blood from her limbs, but her heart ached for him, seemingly alone at the head of his country—trying to be all things to all people.

Not that it should matter to her. To her he was a business associate, nothing more, or so she should continue to remind herself.

She was still thinking of Yusef and his duties—and not necessarily as a business associate—as she lay down on her bed and drifted off to sleep, jet lag and the morning's activities catching up with her. Miryam woke her at six, with a message that His Highness wished to speak with her. He was in the courtyard, Miryam explained, playing with the children.

Playing with the children? Tall, upright, slightly remote Yusef? And wasn't he supposedly so busy? Uncharitable thoughts pushed through Gemma's head as she dressed, not hurrying exactly but aware a summons was a summons, the awe in Miryam's voice as she breathed the words 'His Highness' enough to tell her that.

'He sent this gown.'

Gemma's head was still fuzzy with sleep so the words didn't mean much, but when Miryam spread the emerald-green gown on the bed, the light from the window catching on the golden threads, Gemma's lungs stopped working while her heart beat out a frenzied tattoo.

It doesn't mean anything, her head told her too-excitable body, while to Miryam, who was touching the gown with something akin to reverence, Gemma managed to say calmly, 'Oh, it's the material I admired this morning. How kind.'

But as she slipped the wondrous gown over her head and saw the way the colour brightened her eyes and lit up her hair, her heart continued to believe it was a special gift.

Wanted to believe—for all he'd said anything between them was impossible.

And for all she knew that it was true…

There were women in the courtyard with the children, looking just like the butterflies Yusef had described in their bright silk gowns. And everywhere the children played and tumbled—like nothing more than a litter of puppies. He'd got that right as well!

He sat, bare-headed in the twilight, on the wide loggia outside the big house she now knew was his. The older woman Gemma had met at breakfast was by his side, while Fajella played at his feet, looking up at him from time to time, winning a smile that made Gemma's heart ache just to see it.

The little motherless child, the busy man—how hard it must be for the two to form a bond. From what she'd learned he saw Fajella mostly as she slept—he must seem like a stranger to the little girl.

But as Gemma approached him it was as if invisible strings ran between them. Once again the sensations she'd experienced in the rose garden outside the hospital returned and her skin prickled with awareness of his presence, her blood thickened in her veins as desire threatened to choke her.

Cool, act cool, she told herself, for in spite of his talk of attraction, it was ridiculous to believe he too might be feeling the things she was feeling, although his eyes, as he'd seen her in the gown, had gleamed and she thought she'd seen a tiny nod of acknowledgement.

'Good evening.'

Ultra-cool, but little Fajella looked up at Gemma's voice and gave a crow of delight then started on unsteady legs towards her new friend.

And towards the steps!

Gemma sprang forward to catch the infant before she fell, Yusef also going into action, so the two of them met, hands grasping the child, fingers touching, awareness searing so strongly through Gemma that she *knew* he *had* to feel it.

Her eyes met his and time stood still, the sexual attraction that had flared to life between them with that first kiss sizzling in the air around them so strongly Gemma wondered if the other women in the area could see it, feel it, smell it even, like ozone after lightning!

Or was her over-active imagination colouring the situation? Yusef's voice as he retrieved his child and thanked Gemma was coldly formal, his face so blank she wondered if she'd imagined the flash of desire in his eyes and the whisper of her name on his outgoing breath. He stood there, Fajella hitched on his hip, and looked across the courtyard, apparently catching someone's eye for one of the women came and took his daughter to play with the other children.

'Folly!' Yusef muttered to himself. It had been folly to send for her—to give in to his need to see her again, if only in the company of others, especially see her in the dress that high-lighted so well her vivid beauty. But now she was here, he had to speak to her, to thank her for the way she'd helped the injured, as if that was the only reason he had sent for her. Not by a word or glance could he betray the inexplicable sexual attraction he felt towards this woman, betray the strength of his need to see her, touch her, be near to her. The women of the family would be watching them, and all were sharp enough to spot a secret liaison, even to suspect a hurried kiss.

Not that a hurried kiss with Gemma would ever be enough. He knew that in some deep instinctive way. He would always want more…

'Were there any fatalities in the explosion? Have you heard how those injured are doing?' she asked, settling down on the top step of the loggia as if all her life she'd sat on floors. Knowing he couldn't join her on the step, he resumed his seat beside his father's senior wife, and replied in what he hoped was a suitably regal manner.

'One man was very badly injured, burns to sixty per cent of his body, but we must be thankful that the other injuries were not as severe. Yes, some have bad burns but all were treatable. Some people have other injuries, broken limbs, cuts and bruises, but apparently that end of the market was quiet at the time.'

He watched as she took in what he was telling her, and saw her lips curve into a slight smile.

'Quiet?' she queried. 'I wouldn't like to see it when it was busy.'

He returned her smile—that was acceptable surely. He was handling this well. There'd been a momentary lapse when he'd first seen her, and again when their hands had touched earlier, but he was back in control now.

'But it has thrown your plans out,' she continued. 'I still believe it's important to speak to some of the women before I can make any definite suggestions. Is there some way I can contact Yanne directly to discuss things with her, so you do not need to waste any more time with me?'

Did she really think time spent with her was wasted? Not that he *had* time to spend with her, there was always so much to do, but with Abed returning soon, perhaps—

'Are you listening?'

Her demand was so abrupt his stepmother started, then she looked from him to Gemma and he could see questions forming in her mind.

'Sorry, it's been a long day.' He rushed into an apology. 'I will arrange for Yanne to come here in the morning. She will bring some women from the different tribes.'

Gemma smiled as she thanked him and as the smile stirred something in his chest, he realised he could stay no longer there in front of her—or anywhere in her vicinity—not in public. He stood up.

'You will excuse me, but whenever possible when I am at home it is my custom to read a story and put Fajella to bed at this time. Miryam will look after you.'

Aware he was probably arousing even more suspicion among the women with this abrupt departure, he walked across to where Fajella was crawling up the steps—far more successfully than she'd been heading down them. But to his dismay it wasn't him she sought but the new friend she had found in Gemma.

It had to be the hair—fascinating to a little girl surrounded by black-haired women.

'Perhaps tonight I could read the story,' Gemma suggested, as the little girl gripped her fingers and tugged at her hand.

How could he get out of that one?

Gemma looked up at Yusef, aware something had shifted in their relationship, the air between them charged with static.

He nodded, almost curtly, then reached out to take his daughter from her.

'We can do it together,' he said, and strode away, Gemma following in his wake, unable to work out if he actually wanted a little of her company in private—as she most certainly longed for just a little of his—or if he had suggested it in order to get her alone and perhaps tell her to stay away from his daughter.

Once in Fajella's bedroom, he dismissed Anya, telling her he would send for her when he departed. The little girl chose a book from a pile beside her bed—in Arabic of course—then, to Gemma's surprise, Yusef chose another one, in English, reminding his daughter, in English again, that Gemma wanted to read the story to her.

So Gemma sat on the edge of the cot, the side down, and read a story about a little girl who wanted a pet and a zoo that sent different animals for her to try. It was obvious Fajella knew the story for she followed it, using a tiny forefinger to open up the tabs on each page, revealing the animals behind them. Yusef, meanwhile, leaned negligently against a chest of drawers, surrounded by dolls and bears but looking no less regal and imposing for his surroundings. He said nothing, but Gemma could feel his watchful gaze on her the whole time, for all that he was here to tuck his daughter into bed.

'Your turn,' Gemma said to him as she finished the story, although Fajella was about to fall asleep, her eyelids heavy, her gaze fixed on nothing in particular.

Yusef took Gemma's place on the edge of the cot, and though Gemma knew she should leave the room, the musical cadence of Yusef's voice as he read the other story, and the naked love on his face as he looked down at his daughter, held her spellbound.

The little girl fell asleep and Yusef, stood up, covered the child with a light quilt, pulled up the side of the cot, and adjusted the nightlight until it was nothing more than a faint glow.

Gemma made to leave the room, but his hand on her shoulder halted her. With a gentle but firm grip he turned her, so they stood together in the semi-darkness.

'I am so weak a man it might be best if I cede the title of ruler and let my brother govern our land,' he growled. 'If I am not strong enough to resist an attraction that I know is impossible, how can I show strength in ruling my country?'

The words ground from his lips as if they'd had to push through a lot of resistance to reach the air.

'Not seeing you at all, that's the answer to this thing that has happened between us, but can I do it? No! A minute, an hour out of your company and I am looking for excuses to send for you. It is not good enough!'

He turned away from her and paced the room, fortunately large enough to allow a little pacing.

'I could go home,' Gemma suggested, suspecting he was genuinely upset, probably more at what he saw as a lack of manly strength and moral fibre than at the attraction.

'And leave the job undone? Leave the women and children without access to the full range of medical care they need? You would do that?'

'Not willingly,' Gemma admitted, 'but what do you suggest?'

The broad, white-clad shoulders lifted in an elegant shrug.

'We go on as before. You do your work, we will see each other as part of that, and this attraction—we will take it no further.'

'Good, because this part of "we" has no desire whatsoever to take it further,' Gemma told him, trying for haughty but falling miles short as it was such a bare-faced lie. But the last thing she wanted was for this man to suspect the strength of her attraction to him.

'No?'

A simple word—two letters—rising at the end in a question, yet it sent a shiver of presentiment through Gemma, a shiver that began in her chest and travelled north and south so by the time his lips closed on hers, plundering them with piratical force, she was almost expecting it.

Almost, but not quite, so at first she did nothing, simply stood there and let his lips and tongue do what they would, until heat replaced the shiver and her body sank against his, a pathetic whimper of surrender escaping her lips as she met and matched his fiery intensity.

You cannot have sex with this man in his daughter's bedroom.

The thought lodged in her head, and maybe held the reins that kept their joining to a kiss.

Or did he hold the reins?

Was his control equal to hers—perhaps even stronger?

Could he ever get his fill of her, drink enough of her taste? Yusef wondered, clamping the woman's tall, slim body against his, feeling the softness of her breasts and belly, the spread of her hips, exploring her through kisses.

Was it shameful, to be kissing her in Fajella's bedroom? The infant lay asleep, she would not be disturbed, and no matter how strong his urgency, he would do no more than kiss this woman in this place. To not kiss her had become impossible, and for all his talk of not taking the attraction further, he knew the strength of what lay between them would dictate that at some time, in some place, they would come together.

His ancestors had believed in djinns and other spirits and would have put this madness down to a spell cast by Boudariah the black devil, but he knew it was more basic than that—this spell had to do with the inexplicable chemistry that sometimes occurred between a man and a woman—the chemistry people called attraction.

Though why her, he had no idea.

She pulled away, not abruptly, more to get some air into her lungs, he guessed, for he, too, was feeling breathless.

'Okay, I asked for that,' she whispered, and she rested a hand against his cheek, a gesture that made his heart race faster than her kisses had. 'But I do understand the situation you are in and the dangers of it. I think it's best for both of us if we see each other as little as possible, Yusef. Yanne can pass on any news of my progress, or I could email you a report each day.'

He put his hand on hers to hold it on his cheek and waited for his pulse to slow and his blood to cool.

'It is not what I would wish, but the sensible course,' he said, knowing full well it was the only way forward. Tribal affiliations were flaky at best, his brother's supporters were gathering strength, so the last thing he needed was a scandal of some kind so early in his reign. And an affair with a foreigner *would* cause a scandal but, worse, it would undermine the work *she* was here to do, perhaps devalue it, when it was so important.

Then he kissed her again, a gentler kiss this time, letting his lips tell her of the regret he felt, but not, this time, of the frustration…

'Can you find your way back to the guest house?' he asked, as he moved apart from her once more.

'I can,' she murmured, and he pressed his lips to her forehead.

'Go in peace, then, Gemma Murray. I will sit with Fajella for a while.'

He ushered her out of the door and watched her silent, barefoot walk along the corridor. Then he followed a little way, out of curiosity, and saw her slip on her sandals outside the front door but walk to the guest house not through the courtyard but in the shadows of the wide loggia that ran along the front of the buildings, joining them all.

Back in Fajella's room he squatted beside the cot, watching his sleeping child, thinking of her mother. He wanted a wife so the little one would have a mother, but could he honourably take one when he had failed his first wife so badly?

And could he honourably take a wife when he was so strongly attracted to a red haired foreigner, and in his mind at least could not be faithful to a wife?

He sighed then remembered Abed would return in the morning. Maybe with him here to share the workload and to talk to about the confusion in his mind, he could sort things out.

Maybe—

Gemma woke early after a troubled night's sleep and asked Miryam if it would be rude for her to have some breakfast in the guest house. She used the excuse of having work to prepare for the day's meeting but, in fact, she was reluctant to face the women of Yusef's family, certain they must be wondering about the pair of them taking Fajella to her bed— wondering about the relationship between Yusef and herself.

Not that there was a relationship. His kisses on the plane had been from kindness and it was simply unfortunate that it had awoken a sexual attraction between them that was diffi- cult to resist. But that's all it was, sexual attraction, and if sometimes her heart ached for him, well, that was because she saw the pressure he was under in his role of ruler, and understood some of the dilemmas facing him.

She was up and dressed by the time Miryam brought her breakfast and because what she could see of the day through the fretted arched windows of her room looked inviting, she took her laptop and her breakfast out onto the loggia, where carpets and thick cushions promised comfort in the shade.

There was little she could do before she spoke to Yanne and the other women, but she had a map of Fajabal that had been in the things the secretary had given her back at home. It showed the borders of the country, the waters of the Gulf on one side, a line through desert sands to the south and east, and in the north the broken-looking black mountains she'd seen pictures of while back in Sydney.

And remembering, she gave a start for she'd not thought of the centres since her arrival in Fajabal. Opening up her computer, she got on line and found a number of reassuring emails from the staff of both the houses. Her guilt subsided— of course everything would be all right back home. She sent a belated 'arrived safely' email, assuring the staff she'd be in touch again soon, then returned to her study of the map.

Fajabal was a small country and seemed only to have settlements along the coast, in the city, where she was now, and in isolated spots inland, perhaps oases, though she knew little of the geography of the area.

'You wish to talk here or at the hospital?'

She looked up to see Yanne and five women with her, tribal women from their sturdy clothes and bare heads.

'Will your friends be comfortable here?' Gemma asked, and was surprised when all of the women nodded.

'They all have English,' Yanne told her, correctly interpreting Gemma's surprise. 'As traders and travellers, the nomadic tribes have always spoken many languages.'

'Even the women?' Gemma asked, as Miryam brought out more cushions for the women to sit on, and other servants brought platters of fruit and sweets and pots of coffee, almost as if the group had been expected.

Yanne sat then smiled at Gemma.

'Men may be tougher in war but women are tougher in business,' she said. 'We can bargain better, get better prices for our goods or buy goods more cheaply. It is our way.'

The other women settled themselves, nodding acknowledgement of Yanne's introductions. They accepted tiny cups of coffee and sweetmeats from the platters, and Gemma realised this ceremonial offering and accepting of hospitality must precede any serious talk. But once the coffee pot was dispensed with, the talk began, the women's first concern being for their children.

'We are coming to live in a place where diseases spread quickly. In the desert, in the past, a child might have a runny nose or sometimes a fever, but we hear of all these other things, measles, and chickenpox—these are things city children get. Will our children get them?'

Remembering how such seemingly minor childhood diseases had decimated indigenous populations in the early days of white settlement in Australia and America, Gemma understood the problem. She explained about the vaccines available to protect children against such things.

Some of the women had already had their children vaccinated, but all were interested, so they chattered among themselves, sometimes in English and sometimes in their native tongue, losing Gemma, although every now and then she caught a word that obviously worked in both languages.

'At home in my land we have programmes for vaccinations that begin when the children are babies. Here we could start similar programmes.' Gemma looked around the small circle. 'You would all be willing to have your children vaccinated against things like measles and chickenpox and whooping cough?'

'Many women would fear this,' one woman said, and others nodded.

'We could run a campaign explaining why this is a good idea. We could start with a programme for children who are at school and then move on to the younger children. What is the best way to advertise something like this?'

The women chattered amongst themselves, and offered suggestions that seemed so ordinary to Gemma that she smiled.

'Television, newspapers, magazines and posters on buildings where the women go,' she summed up.

The women smiled and nodded, and Gemma moved the conversation on, telling them about the separate facility at the hospital that Yusef had created.

'Ah, that is good,' one of the women said. 'We do not like going to the other part of the hospital.'

'We do not like seeing men doctors,' another put in. 'Or women doctors who think like doctors instead of thinking like a woman when another woman is in trouble.'

Gemma let the sentence play out in her head and understood what was being said. It was about attitude, something she insisted on in the centres she had started. And suddenly Yusef's insistence on wanting her to look at the services became clear. He wanted more than a medical centre, he wanted a special place for the women and children of his country, and staff they could approach with confidence, staff he wanted Gemma to find and train.

'That is why Wardeh died,' someone else said. 'Trouble with her labour but the man doctor the old highness sent, he was too much a doctor and not enough a person, so he didn't understand she was so distressed.'

There was more excited chatter as they obviously recalled this event, then Yanne explained.

'Wardeh was my sister, Fajella's mother. Her name, it is one of the words we have for the rose, and Yusef planted these roses in her honour.'

Yanne waved her hands towards the glorious display of roses in the courtyard and Gemma felt as if a dagger had slid into her heart as she realised how much he must have loved his wife to have honoured her this way—and to want the reminders of her with him always.

Yes, an affair between them was impossible—she'd accepted that—but had she been harbouring some hope, deep inside, that it might be more than attraction he felt? That it might be love?

Why else would she have felt such a jolt of pain?

CHAPTER NINE

THE talk continued, more coffee coming out, lunch, and snacks, the women slowly opening up about health problems some of them already had, telling Gemma things they would never tell a male doctor, shy even talking of their bodies to her, although the group was now so relaxed they could laugh at each other's embarrassment.

Ideas were forming in Gemma's head—a service based on the centres at home but with more outreach services—a small bus outfitted as a surgery perhaps that went out to the settlements rather than expecting the women to always come to the hospital.

But all the time the scent of the roses hung in the air, like a perfumed ghost, haunting the dark places of her mind.

'Ah, my little one!' Yanne cried out, as the shadows lengthened in the courtyard and tiredness began to blur the edges of Gemma's mind.

She looked up and saw the children were out again, playing by the fountain in the middle of the courtyard, Fajella among them but heading towards the gathering on the guesthouse loggia.

Yanne left the group and went down the steps, picking up the little girl and tossing her in the air.

'So sad,' one of the other women said. 'He married Wardeh, Yusef did, to please his father and she to please her father, to bring the tribes together, but she was not like Yanne, brave and bold. Wardeh was a shy rose, one that flowers in the shadows, but had there been a place like you are speaking of, a medical centre where women feel confident and safe, she might have sought help earlier and lived.'

The words twisted the knife in Gemma's heart. Yusef might say he saw the medical centre as part of a larger restructuring of the overtaxed hospital system, but his passion for it was an attempt to atone for his wife's death.

She was thinking these gloomy thoughts when a tug at the hem of her skirt alerted her to the fact that she had a new visitor. Fajella was standing beside her, a pretty shell in her hand, holding it out to Gemma, offering a gift.

'Oh, thank you, sweetheart,' she said, gathering the little girl to her for a hug and a kiss.

The other women all smiled and some applauded.

'She has taken to you,' one of them said.

'It's my hair,' Gemma told them. 'She hasn't seen anything like it before.'

The women seemed to accept this explanation for now they too talked about Gemma's hair, some of them touching it, one of them showing the red in her own hair.

'Henna,' she said. 'I like to use it.'

The group broke up, Gemma rising, Fajella still in her arms, to say goodbye to them and thank them for their help. She hadn't wanted to take notes while the women were talking for it could have stifled the natural flow of conversation but now there was so much she wanted to get into the computer before she forgot it that she was pleased to see them depart.

She sat again and opened her computer, Fajella settling by her side.

Gemma looked around and saw Anya waiting at the bottom of the steps, but although the nanny called to Fajella the little girl remained where she was.

'I don't mind her staying,' Gemma said. 'She's sitting quietly.'

But what she didn't realise was that it would become a habit, Fajella coming to where Gemma sat in the loggia late each afternoon, settling beside her foreign friend, entertaining herself while Gemma tried to recall all she'd learned during the day, and work it into the larger plan she was making for the new service.

It was exciting, she had to admit it, as the days flew by. So many women wanted to be part of the service, nurses and doctors who had trained overseas, now wanting not only to work in their own country but to be part of an innovative and exciting experiment in community medicine. And their excitement infected Gemma, who found that the hard work helped her forget about Yusef, except in the dark hours of the night when she would see a light on in his big house across the courtyard and picture him, a slight frown on his face, still working.

But for the most part she was happy with the way the plans were developing, and even happier, when, each afternoon, she took some time off from the complex logistics of the new service to play in the rose garden with Fajella. If the other women in the compound wondered about the attachment that had grown between the two of them, they said nothing, although the older woman, the senior wife, as Gemma thought of her, stopped Gemma one day to thank her for the time she spent with the little girl.

'She was too quiet—too withdrawn—this child, and her father, he doesn't have the time to play with her. Not now when things are difficult for him and there is unrest in our land.'

Gemma would have loved to ask more—about Yusef's difficulty, not about Fajella—for she suspected the older brother Yusef had spoken of, was probably this woman's son. Whose side, then, was this woman on?

But Fajella's cry of greeting interrupted their conversation and Gemma thanked the older woman and turned to welcome the little girl.

Now much steadier on her feet, she came racing along a path beneath an arch of brilliant red roses and, knowing the game she expected, Gemma chased after her, pretending to be trying to catch up, Fajella squealing her delight. They had just rounded a corner in the arched arbour, when Yusef appeared.

Although Gemma was in touch with him via email, she hadn't seen him since the evening in Fajella's bedroom when he'd cursed his weakness in not being able to stay away from her. Well, he'd got over that successfully enough, though now she saw him and she felt a pang of concern for how tired and drawn he looked.

'They told me I might find my daughter here,' he said, seizing Fajella in his arms and tossing her lightly into the air. 'Seduced away from her father by a red-haired witch.'

Although the words were spoken lightly Gemma had the distinct impression that he wasn't joking. But what could she say? She'd grown to love the little girl, and playing with her provided relief from the stresses of the service she was trying to set up.

And from the heartache of not seeing him—

Then Yusef's eyes met hers above the little girl's head and the hunger Gemma read in them found an immediate response in her body.

'Tomorrow is Friday, our holiday, as you now know,' he said, 'and I, the ruler, am decreeing no work for you. Abed will call for you at nine. It is time you saw the something of our country, especially the sea. You have a swimsuit with you?'

Gemma tried to respond but her heart was beating so rapidly she could barely breathe.

Abed is collecting you, she reminded herself as she nodded a response. And bring a swimsuit! So it is not a private tryst he is suggesting, but at least she'd get to spend some time with Yusef, to feel him close, to look at him when Abed and others were distracted.

Except that a private tryst was exactly what it turned out to be, Abed collecting her as promised, delivering her to a place far out of the city, where high-prowed dhows were moored in rows along a wharf. The driver stopped the car and Abed escorted her to the third in the row, a smaller vessel but still a graceful, dark-timbered boat with a twirling symbol painted on its prow, the reddish-tan triangle of sail already raised.

'Are you as fearful of the sea as you are of the air?' Yusef was dressed in faded jeans and a black polo shirt, barefoot—piratical. The gleam in his eyes told Gemma he was teasing, and as Abed said goodbye and the pirate helped her on board, she forgot all the reasons she shouldn't be spending time alone with this man, and went straight into his arms.

No kisses just a tight embrace, holding each other close, no need for more, an unspoken agreement between them that more—should there be a more—could wait till later.

Neither had she any qualms, feeling a certain rightness in this stolen time together, knowing it could, in the future, be a very treasured memory.

'Now I have to cast off,' he finally murmured, breaking away from her but keeping hold of her hand. Gemma followed him down the length of the craft, waiting while he threw the rope ashore, then did the same at the prow before releasing the sail and adjusting it so the light breeze filled it and they drifted silently away from the wharf.

'The sea *is* turquoise,' Gemma whispered, afraid if she spoke too loudly the bubble of delight that was wrapped around them would surely burst.

'And the sand is white, for all the black stone of the mountains,' Yusef said, tugging her towards him so they sat together in the sunken cockpit, one of his hands holding the rope that moved the sail, the other clasping hers. 'We are going to my island.'

'*Your* island?' Gemma queried, and he laughed.

'One of the only perks I've yet discovered about this highness business,' he said. 'An island where only the ruler can go. Originally it was a place where he met with the gods to get advice or maybe orders, and through the ages it has retained some special significance so only the ruler and those he chooses to accompany him can set foot there.'

'Privacy at last,' Gemma muttered, disconcerted by the mix of emotions she was experiencing. Yes, she was excited, physically excited, about being alone with Yusef, but what was the point of them spending the day together—and sharing whatever pleasure the day might bring—when nothing could come of their relationship?

'You don't yearn for that?' he asked, picking up on the sarcasm in her voice.

Gemma sighed.

'Yes, I'd be lying if I said I didn't,' she admitted, 'but aren't we making things harder for ourselves? Wouldn't it be easier to make a clean break? In fact, didn't we do that? Haven't we managed to avoid seeing each other the last few weeks?'

'Is that what you want?'

Gemma turned towards him and saw the concern in his dark eyes. She shrugged, a helpless gesture. 'Not necessarily what I want,' she told him, and brushed a kiss across his lips. 'But given that there's no point in taking our attraction further, isn't it the sensible thing to do?'

He kissed her back, but swiftly for they were out in a channel now and the wind was frisky.

'Then let's not be sensible—at least, not for today,' he said, before concentrating solely on the sail. 'Let us be as unsensible as it is possible to be! And maybe, just maybe,' he added softly, 'there *might* be a point in taking the attraction further. I have an idea. Just you wait and see!'

He brought the boat ashore in a narrow inlet, beaching it on, yes, white sand between high, jagged rock walls that reached out into the sea. Beyond the beach, green grass and stunted trees grew in what looked like a hidden valley—a secret place.

Yusef helped her clamber out, and led her across the sand. At the top of the beach a picnic had already been set up, a carpet spread in a patch of shade, thick cushions thrown around on it, a brazier with a coffee pot on it, and a wicker basket promising an array of delights to eat.

Gemma sank down among the pillows, and sighed with the sheer delight of it.

'Coffee?'

'Does his highness actually serve the coffee or are a troupe of servants about to appear out of the bushes?'

Yusef smiled, and only now, as he felt his body relax at her teasing, did he realise how tense he'd been.

'No servants,' he said, sitting down beside her then leaning back so he lounged among the cushions.

'Then no coffee,' she whispered, and the restraint he'd been practising for what seemed like for ever broke and he took her in his arms, holding her close, kissing her pale lips, tasting the strawberries again.

And for long, long minutes kissing was enough, learning her through taste and touch, but soon, knowing the dhow shielded them from any possibility of being seen from the water, and that the island was completely uninhabited, he began to undress her, delighting in her response, in the shivers that ran across her skin as he drew off her shirt, the goose-bumps that formed when he kissed her now naked neck.

She slid her hands beneath his shirt, splaying her fingers across his chest, pressing into his flesh as if to steady herself while he continued his tender assault.

Gemma wondered if hearts could burst, so fast was hers beating. Yusef was stripping her with gentle but persistent efficiency, and his actions, not to mention the kisses accompanying them, were firing her to a heated desire she'd never felt before.

His long, strong fingers explored her body, awakening it to magical sensations. She could hear the little cries she gave, counterpoint to the shushing of wavelets on the beach, then urgency fired both of them, and she was touching him as well, touching him with the same licence he was using on her.

'We have all day,' he reminded her, but patience had no part to play this sunlit morning. His hands and mouth signalled urgency and Gemma's body screamed for more than tender touches, so clothes were now shed willy-nilly and once naked, he held her to him, so skin met skin. He kissed her lips, looked into her eyes, and accepted the invitation of eyes and hands, sliding deep inside her, their bodies joined, adjusting, then moving, moving, moving, lost in the chorus of delight that fluttered from their lips.

It became a battle, Gemma holding out, not wanting to reach a climax until she knew Yusef, too, was ready, but he teased her and built the pressure higher and higher until, with a flash of sensation so riveting she shuddered again and again, her moment came, her body clenching, finally breaking *his* control so both were spent.

Now they ate, Yusef feeding her grapes.

'Like the goddesses painted on ancient vases,' she said, and he bent and kissed her grape-wet lips.

'It was the gods who were fed, you lazy woman. You should be doing this for me.'

She reached up and touched her forefinger to his lips.

'You don't get enough pampering?'

He nodded, but she saw the smile slide from his face and realised for all the multitude of servants he might have, he probably *didn't* get enough pampering. Not private, personal pampering.

Now she sat up and pushed him back among the cushions.

'So it's my job, is it?'

She took the bunch of grapes from his hand but, rather than feed him, she set them back in the picnic basket and searched in the big handbag she'd brought with her, coming up with a tube of hand cream.

She squeezed some on her hands then spread it on his shoulders, massaging it in, pushing her thumbs into the tight tendons at the back of his neck and pressing against the pressure points at the base of the skull.

'To do this properly you need to roll over,' she told him, and when he did, she straddled his back, naked and unashamed for there was something out of time and space in this encounter and they were in a magical place. Spreading more cream, she massaged his shoulders, finding more pressure points and kneading them until he squirmed with the pain.

'I know it's good for me, it feels good and bad at the same time, but enough's enough.'

His voice was muffled by the pillows, and Gemma moved her hands lower, running her thumbs up and down the side of his spine, sitting now on his buttocks, delighting in the freedom he was allowing her—the freedom of his body!

His beautiful body!

Her fingers slid around his ribs, and felt a scar.

'An accident?' she asked, still massaging.

'An operation.'

Her hands stilled and she tried to work it out.

'It's not appendicitis, wrong place for a scar. What happened?'

'I gave Abed a kidney.'

He said it as easily as she might have said she'd offered a friend a biscuit.

'You *gave* Abed a kidney?'

He turned over now, tipping her off his back but catching her so they lay close again.

'He had a bad form of nephritis as a child and neither of his kidneys worked too well. In our twenties we decided to look for a donor and it turned out I was a good match.'

'Which means you only have one kidney now,' Gemma said, wondering why her heart was beating out a panicky rhythm.

'We have one working kidney each and one is all anyone needs,' he said, so calmly the panicky rhythm eased a little. 'In fact, research done on thousands of living kidney donors has found that our lives run on exactly the same lines as non-donors. The kidney that is left actually grows and takes up eighty to ninety per cent of the work the two kidneys once did, so there is no danger.'

'No danger?' Gemma said. 'But don't you have to treat it carefully because it *is* the only one?'

'And how does one treat a kidney well?' he teased. 'Are you aware of any action you take to protect your kidneys? Anyway, you can be sure that I am always careful,' he said, and began to kiss her again, but Gemma's mind was on the operation. Presumably this had all happened well before anyone had known Yusef would end up as the country's ruler, or surely he wouldn't have been allowed to go through with the donation. And often the donor suffered more than the recipient in the post-operative stage, Gemma having seen this situation during her general training.

'You're not with me in these kisses,' Yusef complained, pushing up to lounge on one elbow. 'Perhaps a swim?'

Of course people with one kidney could lead normal lives, Gemma chided herself, but now she knew this she found herself worrying about him. Would the water be too cold? If he got a chill could it affect his kidney—?

'Come,' he said, hauling her to her feet. 'Do you think I didn't go through all you're thinking when I did it? I was a medical student at the time and knew enough to be able to imagine the most appalling consequences, but the truth is as long as it isn't damaged by disease or accident, my one kidney is perfectly adequate. And disease or accident could carry me away anyway, even if I had the full complement of kidneys.'

Gemma knew he was right, and that her sudden spurt of anxiety was totally stupid, but that didn't stop the little knot of worry that stayed planted in her head.

She followed him down the beach and into the warm, clear water, feeling it wrap around her, cleansing and supporting her. She lay on her back and kicked her legs, feeling her hair float round her head like seaweed, wondering how the sexually shy and slightly prudish Gemma she had been had suddenly been transformed into this creature frolicking naked in the water.

With a man!

But what a man!

He swam with long clean strokes out to the entrance of the inlet, then back again, swimming because he enjoyed the freedom of it, Gemma guessed, out here, away from all the pressures of his position. And that there were pressures she knew, for even after they'd made love, the strain and tension remained etched into his face.

'Sex in the water?'

He'd bobbed up beside her, a wide grin chasing away the lines she thought she'd seen.

She felt her face colour and knew the shy and prudish Gemma wasn't totally gone, but now he was touching her, and before long the concept he'd suggested became not only clear but strangely exciting as well.

CHAPTER TEN

AFTER the swim, he offered her a clean *wezaar*, the white cloth he wrapped around his waist beneath his gown. She tied it, sarong-style, around her body, knotting it above her breasts. Then, covered well enough to not feel embarrassed, Gemma followed him along a narrow path into the green valley.

It was beautiful, moss and lichen growing on stones in what might, when it rained, be a tiny creek. More rocks formed a waterfall, dry now but greenly beautiful with delicate, dangling ferns.

'There must be enough water retained in the rocks to keep the plants growing,' Yusef said, and Gemma realised he was as intrigued by the place as she was.

'You haven't been here before?'

He shook his head.

'I didn't have the right to come,' he explained. 'I don't know if my father ever used the island, but if he did, he certainly didn't bring any of his children along or I'd have heard.'

They'd climbed the rocky fall and reached a high point from where they could look out over the sea and back towards the mainland.

'It's beautiful,' Gemma breathed, sitting down on a large rock to drink in the view.

'And you, too, are beautiful,' Yusef told her, taking her hand and holding it in a tight clasp. 'So beautiful I cannot give you up. I have thought,' he continued, 'about our situation, and it seems to me there is a simple answer.'

He'd been speaking slowly, as if thinking out each word, and quite softly, so when the words did come Gemma wasn't certain she'd heard them right.

'A simple answer?' she echoed.

'Very simple,' he said, dropping a light kiss on the back of her fingers, 'although it would mean big changes in your life and it might not be so simple in your way of thinking, in Western thinking. Here it would be quite acceptable for you to be my mistress, to have a house I would provide for you within the compound. Financially you would be secure for ever, even should you find in time the arrangement doesn't suit you and you decide you wish to leave, although I would hope that wouldn't happen.'

Gemma eased her hand away from his and battled to make sense of what he'd just proposed.

'Let me get this right,' she said, moving as far away from him as she could on the tiny plateau. She slammed her hands on her hips and glared down at him. 'Ever since we got here, every time we've stolen a kiss, you've been telling me that an affair between us could cause such a scandal the people would throw you off the throne, now you're proposing to set me up as your mistress and that's okay? Have I got it straight?'

He frowned at her and shook his head but when he spoke, his words denied the head shake.

'It is understood in all cultures that men have mistresses,' he said. 'This would not be a scandal.'

'But it would be a scandal if it was just an affair? Wouldn't it be the same? Wouldn't I be your mistress if we were having an affair?' Gemma persisted, growing more angry by the second.

He held out his hands in a helpless gesture—about as helpless as a lion guarding his prey, Gemma guessed.

'An affair—it smacks of something not exactly underhand but shifty or illicit, whereas to take a mistress, well, that is not so different from taking another wife. My father, although he only had the allowed four wives at any one time, kept many mistresses.'

'Oh, well, if your father did it, that *must* make it all right!' Gemma retorted. 'And just how many wives and mistresses are you planning on having?'

'You're making a mockery of it now,' Yusef growled. 'Do you not see I am serious?

'Serious about taking a mistress, and a foreign mistress, at that? That's okay, is it? That's not going to wreck the succession? That's not going to tip the scales should your brother decide to force you off the throne?'

Yusef sighed, banking down the anger that had risen to replace his original disappointment. Gemma was angry enough for both of them, although he couldn't fathom why. In his head it had seemed the ideal solution. He had mapped it all out.

But in practice it had not gone at all the way he'd hoped. Well, the first part of the day had, it had been stupendously successful, but now he had this woman even more firmly ensnared in his blood, she was being difficult.

Impossible!

He tried for patience. Began again.

'You do not like the idea?'

'I hate the idea,' she snapped. 'And so should you! What's wrong with you, to be thinking this way? Has this highness business gone to your head? You're a caring man for all the power you wield, yet you'd offer me some kind of—of dishonourable position in your life. And what of Fajella? What of your daughter? How, as she grows up, do you explain me to her?'

And with that the woman with whom he had been inexorably falling in love stormed away, scrambling down the gully and disappearing into the green grove of trees.

Gemma slipped and slid, her mind whirling with too many thoughts and emotions for her to separate them. She tried to analyse how she felt. Maybe if she could sort out her physical state then her mind would fall into order later. She'd start with the heaviness in her chest, where her heart, which had only recently admitted its love for this man, was now clumped like a lump of lead.

Heavier, if anything!

Why?

She gave a scoffing huff of laughter.

She could answer that one. It was because the man you thought just might love you—though why you thought that, who knows—has just positively proven he doesn't, by asking you to be his mistress!

Yusef heard her crashing progress down the gully. What now?

They were stuck together on a deserted island.

She was probably thinking he'd abandon her there if she didn't agree.

Gemma's response had startled him. She'd been so responsive—so warm and loving and utterly wonderful in his arms, so generous in her love-making—that her reaction to his suggestion had come as a total shock.

Had he misread the situation as far as the word 'mistress' was concerned? Here the women in these positions enjoyed a better position than a wife—with far fewer responsibilities.

He had understood similar situations were accepted in the Western world but maybe the word had different connotations in Australia?

He followed her down towards the beach, reaching the picnic spot, which he'd set up with such care and excitement earlier that morning. Now it looked far less romantic.

Particularly with a tall, red-headed woman sitting straight-backed, cross-legged and arms folded in the middle of the carpet.

'It seems I must apologise,' he said, sounding stiff and stilted for he still didn't understand. 'If I have embarrassed you I am sorry, but let us put it behind us and enjoy the rest of the day. We will eat and talk of other things,' he told her, although in his head he wanted to yell at her, to demand to know what was so bad about his suggestion. What use was his power as ruler if he couldn't take a mistress should he wish to?

She settled on the cushions, close enough for him to touch, but at least he had the fortitude to not touch—not right now. They ate and talked of other things, the history of his people, the nomadic tribes now calling Fajabal home, the sorry state of a world where there was always war somewhere.

Then suddenly, surprisingly, she reached out and touched his scar.

'You must have loved Abed very dearly to have done so much for him,' she said, her voice soft, her eyes looking at him but not, he thought, seeing him.

'We are brothers in the truest sense, though not by blood,' Yusef told her honestly, thinking of how having Abed by his side had got him through some tough and lonely years.

'Maybe if I'd had a sibling,' she said quietly, 'someone to show me love, then this would all be easier.'

Gemma turned so she could look out past the dhow towards the sea as the words spilled out.

'But because there *was* no one, for a long time I assumed I was unlovable—my grandfather and later the man I thought I loved, neither of them loving me—but I've matured enough to know that's not right, to know that like everyone in the world, I deserve love.'

Yusef shifted slightly and she turned to face him.

'That's why I won't be your mistress—why I won't be second best. It took me a long time to work out that accepting second best just wasn't good enough, and I'm not going to go back on it now.'

What could he say? Offer marriage and risk chaos in his country? She seemed to understand he couldn't do that, for she wasn't asking it of him. And, strangely, although she was refusing his offer, she was now kissing him, kissing him gently at first but with increasing passion, taking the lead in their love-making with firm insistence, so he could only follow where she led, revelling in the erotic sensations she aroused in his body, following her as the pace increased until they rocked and gasped and fought each other for the ultimate release, a wild storm of physical delight that left them depleted, beached on the rug amid the cushions, as still as driftwood flung up on the shore.

Nothing more was said about the proposition and though Yusef felt a little foolish for having assumed she'd accept—and definitely put out that she'd turned him down—he set his feelings aside to make the best of what was left of the day. They swam again, and talked of the plans for the mobile clinics and for vaccination programmes for the children, even talked of Fajella and what lay in her future as far as schooling was concerned.

'Maybe one day she'll be running the clinic, or setting up

new health services,' Gemma said. Was she aware she'd ruined the day when she'd turned him down? Was this chatter her way of pretending all was well between them? 'Who knows where fate will lead a child?'

'I thought fate was more influential in our way of life than in yours,' he said, and saw pain flash across her face.

'When you grow up without your parents, you have to believe in fate, otherwise you blame yourself,' she said, turning to face him with her arms full of bright cushions for they were packing up to leave. 'And believing in fate gets you through bad times—you reason that although it might be picking on you now, surely it must have something better saved up for you in the future.'

He took the cushions out of her arms and drew her close, thinking of the tragic loss she'd suffered.

'And did it?' he asked huskily, and Gemma looked up at him and smiled then rested her head on his shoulder as she said, 'It took a while, but eventually. The success of the centres, me getting involved with them, that's been a huge reward. Even coming here, to this magical place, that's special.'

Yusef brushed his hand over her wet and tangled hair, and felt something shift inside his chest. Never had he met a woman so unselfish, so giving of herself for others, and seeing the success of her own efforts as enough reward. Could it be love he felt for her?

And if it *was* love, then wasn't it a good thing she'd turned down his proposition? One didn't love one's mistress…

She eased out of his arms and picked up the cushions he'd dropped, carrying them down to the dhow, then she returned and, turning her back, pulled on her clothes, signalling the day was over, the magic of it gone…

Was she mad, refusing his offer? Gemma pondered as she

pulled on the loose trousers she'd had specially made for her adventure in Fajabal. Turning down an offer to stay on in this fabulous land? Turning down an offer of security for life?

All because she wanted some ephemeral thing called love?

She shrugged off the questions, because there were no answers. Yusef didn't love her—*couldn't* love her—and that was that.

They sailed back to the mainland, Abed appearing as if by magic as they docked.

'I phoned him earlier,' Yusef explained, seeing her surprise.

'Of course,' Gemma said. 'You do tend to think of everything.'

'Not quite everything,' he said, so sombre that for a moment she wondered if he'd been expecting her to agree to his proposition and was disappointed.

Maybe just a little disappointed, she decided as he touched her lightly on the shoulder by way of farewell. But that was probably more to do with the fact that he was used to getting his own way than with her refusing him.

'Go with Abed, he will take you safely home.'

Gemma turned and looked at the man who was, in fact, saying goodbye. There was so much she wanted to say to him, but there were no words for the emotions tangled inside her chest. She nodded her acceptance of his farewell, and moved towards Abed, feeling the strings she'd always felt between herself and Yusef breaking, one by one, hearing the echoes of their twanging in her mind…

It was a blessing that she was so busy, so caught up in setting up the women's health service she had no time to dwell on the emotional storm she'd thrust into the very darkest corner of her mind. There was enough angst back there for it to hide, so much pain and desertion that one more lot hardly mattered.

What did matter was getting the service right. She knew from experience that the whole operation would be useless and the women wouldn't use it unless she got it right.

In her endeavours, she'd found a champion in Yanne, who had turned up at the hospital one day and announced she'd come to work.

'I have given the stall to my cousin, it is time she learned to run it. I will be your manager here.'

Gemma didn't hesitate to welcome her, assuring her she could have the job. Yanne may not have typing skills, or know her way around the internet, but she knew the women the clinic would serve, and Gemma could hire other people to type, and chase up references and information on the internet.

So it was with Yanne that she first explored the desert sands Yusef had spoken of with love and longing, and though she felt pain as she stared out at the golden dunes, she hoped she hid it well.

Their second trip into the desert, three weeks after her visit to the island, brought them to the camel breeders' camp, an area the size of a football field covered with big black tents. Yanne yelled a greeting and dark-visaged men with odd, folded turbans on their heads called back to her, apparently in welcome for she and Yanne were soon sitting by a fire, drinking strong tea, camel butter floating in it.

Gemma was wondering how much of it politeness would insist she drink when a woman came hurrying towards them, calling out to Yanne, her hands moving in the air as if illustrating whatever she was saying.

'So, we are here, our first mobile clinic, for a birth,' Yanne said to Gemma. 'Come, you will see now how it happens.'

The woman led the way to a smaller tent right at the edge of the encampment.

'It is the birthing place,' Yanne explained. 'Like the room I suggested we set aside in the women's house at the old palace.'

They ducked inside the tent, and found the woman in labour squatting in the middle of it, her hands clenched on a tightly bound bundle of reeds that curved like a new moon and hung suspended by leather straps from the frame of the tent. Two women crouched, one on either side of the straining woman, each holding down one of the woman's heels.

'It gives an anchor for her body, holding her like this,' Yanne said, and as they watched the baby slid into view, a third woman not assisting at all but catching the newborn. 'The baby must make his own way out, it is the custom because it proves his strength and cleverness,' Yanne explained.

Gemma nodded, then couldn't believe it when the woman who had caught the child, handed it, wrapped in black swaddling clothes, to her, smiling and nodding at Gemma, urging her to take the gift.

'It is good luck to have a stranger hold the baby, but only for a short time. Now the mother will suckle him and she will stay here for forty days, while these other women care for her and for the baby so the mother gets plenty of rest.'

Forty days—it was a set period of time that recurred again and again in history, a period of time that existed in stories and beliefs in all cultures. She thought of the young mothers who, these days, often had to go back to work within weeks of having their child, and the stories of some peasant women who gave birth in field, wrapped the infant onto their back and kept working. No forty days of rest for them.

'Will you thank them for me,' she said to Yanne, 'for letting me experience something so special.'

Yanne rattled off the thanks and they left the camp, Gemma feeling again the tug of longing for a child of her own…

Yusef's child?

He was the only man she'd ever love, she knew that now, so...

Returning, weary and travel-stained to the compound, Gemma bathed, then, wrapped in one of the indigo gowns she had grown to love, she sat down to compose a report to send to him, a report, laying out all she'd seen and learned and how the plans were developing with each new experience. A practical report, although she remembered him once talking of poetry and wished it could be otherwise.

Emailing it, she checked on emails from home, then considered going to the women's house to see if Fajella was still awake—perhaps read her a story.

Or are you hoping to run into Yusef? her head demanded, putting a stop to that plan.

Had she been wrong to turn him down? Was she foolish to have dreams of love?

She knew enough of the ways of Fajabel now to know that marrying Yusef was impossible, quite apart from the scandal it would cause and the unrest it could provoke. Marriages here were arranged, and most were political, the marriage of two people bringing together tribes in a political alliance.

So her heart would have to ache—for him and his little daughter and for her own loss—and she would learn to live with it and trust in fate, and a lot of hard work, to provide a wondrous success with the women's and children's centre so the excitement of that success would help ease her pain.

These thoughts haunted her as she went to bed, and stayed with her through the night so her sleep was restless, her body remembering the bliss it had shared with Yusef's, her mind twisting and turning through a maze that had no end.

So she was pleased when the phone by her bed rang just

before daybreak, releasing her from the trap her thoughts had woven.

'I need a doctor. Can you come?'

Abed's voice, and enough urgency in it for her to react immediately.

'Of course,' she said, springing out of bed, wondering where, and when, and why, but answering his desperation.

'I'll pick you up in fifteen minutes, you know the helipad at the back of the palace.'

'Helipad?'

Gemma's echo was so faint Abed would probably not have heard it, but he'd hung up anyway, the phone going dead in her hands.

Helipad?

He was going to take her in a helicopter?

He was asking her to fly?

She couldn't do it, but she had to dress and meet him there anyway. Maybe he was just flying in and from here they'd go by car to wherever it was.

Gemma was brushing her teeth, bundling her hair into a knot and wrapping a scarf around it, washing her face and dragging on clothes while fearful questions circled in her head.

A helicopter?

It must have been the tenth time it repeated itself that the real issue struck her—it wasn't the helicopter she should be worrying about but the fact that Abed needed a doctor. For whom?

And why her, when his brother was a doctor?

CHAPTER ELEVEN

THE helicopter landed as Gemma hurried towards the helipad, clutching her scarf as the downdraught threatened to snatch it away. Abed climbed out as soon as the skids touched down, ducking under the still turning blades.

'It's Yusef,' he said, taking Gemma's arm and hustling her towards the little aircraft, and with those two words killed Gemma's determination to remain on stable ground. 'This is our rescue aircraft and I fly it often, volunteering, but I can't get a doctor from the hospital for no one must know.'

He was yelling this in her ear, against the muted roar of the engines, but as he pushed Gemma up into a seat, he motioned to a headset and she put it on, understanding that they could talk more easily through the device.

Yusef needed a doctor but Abed couldn't use one from the hospital? And a helicopter? Where was Yusef? Was he even alive?

It seemed to take for ever for Abed to regain his seat at the controls, and lift the little craft into the air, Gemma locking her hands in a death grip on the seat. Now he put on his headset and Gemma could ask questions—but what to ask first?

'Yusef?'

Abed shook his head and Gemma read the pain and worry on his face.

'There was an argument. He usually handles things better but lately he's been unsettled, tense, upset.'

Abed didn't add 'since the day at the island' but Gemma felt it in the air between them.

'Yesterday a meeting with his brother escalated into argument and in the end, to clear the air, Yusef suggested they go out to the desert, fly the falcons for a while. It was a sport we all enjoy but he gets little time these days.'

'Falcons?'

She was back to echoing again.

'Hunting birds, but that's beside the point. Yusef didn't come back. Hassim, his brother, swears he left him with the falconer, but the falconer tells me he caged the birds and drove away while the others were still there.'

'What others?' Gemma asked, anxiety coiling like a spring in her stomach.

'Hassim and Maka, who is Hassim's shadow brother. You know about that?'

Gemma nodded, then turned towards Abed as she realised what he suspected.

'You think they might have harmed him? Injured Yusef?'

Abed looked grim.

'I cannot see it of Hassim, no matter how much Hassim might want the crown, but Maka, he is a strange man. He has affiliations with the oil world that I suspect are more lucrative than straightforward business deals would be.'

A chill settled around the coiled spring in Gemma's body, and she peered out at the endless dunes rolling away below them like a golden sea.

'But where can we look? How can we find him, just the

two of us? Shouldn't there be a full-scale search? Can't this man be made to talk?'

'I don't want to start a panic,' Abed told her. 'If the press knew he was missing, maybe dead, there would not only be an outpouring of speculation and misinformation but the power struggle that has been going on beneath the surface would erupt. Although the people's respect for Yusef and his policies is growing every day, and the people grow to love him, they are still in wait-and-see mode as far as his ability to rule is concerned. The last thing he needs right now is a media circus.'

'You know where he's likely to be?' Gemma asked, thinking they should forget the publicity angle and have a fleet of aircraft looking for him.

'I know the area he likes to fly the falcons—and we should be able to see his vehicle.'

And that was that, Abed now concentrating on flying the machine, Gemma realising that one fear can cancel out another, for her mind was totally focussed on finding Yusef now, although she was resolute in not looking out the window of the helicopter.

'Now, start looking. A black Range Rover.'

'Aren't they all?' Gemma muttered, and she tightened her grip on the seat, told her stomach to behave, and peered out through the window. For a moment the world tilted crazily, her head swimming with the old terror, but finding Yusef was far more important than falling apart over a flight, so she steeled herself and looked again, peering down onto the waves of red-gold sand dunes, seeing ahead of them the outline of the rugged black rocky mountains.

'We won't see the car against the rocks,' she said, despairing how they'd ever find anyone in this sea of sand.

'When the sun gets higher the shadows will shift,' Abed told her, sweeping the helicopter this way then that, dropping lower and lower all the time, until the downdraaught sent sand spinning into the air and they had to rise again to get a clearer view.

They spotted the vehicle an hour later, when Gemma was beginning to despair and Abed was muttering about fuel problems. It was parked close to the rocky mountains, barely visible, almost hidden. Abed brought the helicopter into land about a hundred metres away, explaining that if he'd landed closer, the vehicle and anyone near it would be buried in sand from the downdraft.

Gemma fumbled out of her seat belt, hauled off the headset, then wondered exactly what emergency supplies this helicopter carried. Turning around earlier, she'd seen a stretcher locked in behind her seat, so surely there'd be the regular emergency kits most rescue services carried.

'I'll get the bag,' Abed said, helping her out then opening a door into the rear compartment.

He hoisted a large backpack onto his back and led her towards where they'd seen the vehicle, although it was now hidden behind a dune. She struggled through the sand, wondering how Abed could walk so easily, carrying the big load, but when she topped the dune and saw the car, fear for Yusef lent her strength and she hurried forward.

The vehicle was empty, keys in the ignition and a full water bottle sitting on the front passenger seat.

'Wherever he is, he's probably dehydrated by now,' she muttered to herself, grabbing up the bottle. Abed had left the pack by the car and was walking towards the base of the cliffs, calling Yusef's name.

He was in the cleft, lying awkwardly but conscious, for on seeing Abed he spoke to him in his own language.

'He knew I'd come,' Abed translated for her, although drag marks in the sand behind Yusef's supine body suggested he hadn't been entirely certain.

Now she moved forward into Yusef's view.

'Gemma?'

The throaty, tortured word struck like a knife wound in her heart, but now was not the time for personal pain—he was alive and it was her job to make sure he stayed that way. And though she longed to ask what had happened, she didn't, checking his pulse, his blood pressure, his pupils, seeing the contusion on the side of his head, wondering about fluid building up inside his skull, a haematoma waiting to kill him…

'Give him little sips of water,' she told Abed, 'but only little sips.'

She continued to examine him, seeing bruises on his chest, large and heavy—he'd been kicked?'

'Maybe broken pelvis,' Yusef told said, his voice so weak and thready, she shushed him into silence, but as she ran her hands around his hips she could feel something wrong with the integrity of the pelvic ring.

'Yet you tried to move!' Gemma grumbled. 'And how do you know it's not your spine? A broken spine can show the same characteristics.'

She had her fingers on his wrist again. His pulse was a little fast but not thready—dehydration the cause, she guessed.

'Look at my left leg, splayed out like that.' His voice might be weak but there was spirit in the words. 'And if it was spine you'd expect nerve damage, and the sciatic nerve is fine, I can move my legs even if it hurts.'

Gemma was using her hands, still trying to feel the damage, but the jeans he was wearing prevented her from seeing his pelvic region and removing his clothes just wasn't an option.

If there was a broken bone in his pelvis, any movement could cause more damage. She could picture the bone stabbing into his kidney, or slicing through a major blood vessel. Already there could be severe internal bleeding, although he would probably not be conscious if that was the case.

'We've got to move you,' she said, feeling helpless because movement posed such risk.

'Stretcher, pull me on by my clothes. Jeans should keep the pelvic girdle more or less in place.'

He spoke so calmly Gemma could only stare at him, torn between rushing to do exactly as he'd said and bursting into tears, so relieved was she that he was safe.

Well, nearly safe.

Abed left to get the stretcher, Gemma hurrying with him as far as the vehicle to get some fluid and IV equipment from the bag. Pain relief—she'd need to give him something before they moved him, and she sorted through the options, then jogged back. But before she could set up the IV, Yusef caught her hand.

'You flew?' he asked.

'How else was I supposed to find you?' she growled. 'Stupid man that you are! Abed was sure you must be injured and didn't want a doctor from the hospital because it would cause a fuss—word would get out—people might panic.'

'But *you* flew?' Yusef repeated, and Gemma didn't answer, knowing her actions had been a dead giveaway of her love for him. But if it wasn't said out loud it would be less embarrassing, she decided, pulling the IV tubing and catheter out of its packaging.

'Just lie still,' she told him, but again he stopped her, grasping her hand once more.

'It wasn't Hassim,' he said, but Abed had returned and now Gemma slid the needle into her patient's vein, connected the tubing, fitted the bag of fluid, and started it dripping into him. Then an injection of morphine, enough to make him woozy and hopefully enough to make him sleep. She didn't know where the conversation had been going but she guessed he was exonerating his brother.

Why?

The whole thing was a mystery but Yusef had been badly kicked and beaten and someone was responsible.

Tugging him onto the stretcher, using his clothes to move him, she and Abed got Yusef strapped into place, then together carried him back as far as the vehicle.

'Put him in and drive or carry him?' Abed asked.

Gemma hesitated for only a second.

'Carry him,' she said. 'It's not that far and I can manage. Putting him in the vehicle, we might jolt him more than carrying him.'

Yusef was objecting blearily, telling Gemma to put him down, but she ignored his drugged comments and continued towards the helicopter, where she helped Abed slide the stretcher in, then strap it down.

'What now?' she asked Abed, as he shut the rear door on their patient. 'If it is his pelvis he's likely to need surgery or at the very least bed rest. People will have to know.'

'I'll fly him directly to the hospital. Now we know he is safe we can let it be known there's been an accident. Who should we have standing by as far as medical staff are concerned?'

Gemma thought about it.

'A neurologist and an orthopaedic surgeon definitely. Tell them head injury and a suspected fracture of the pelvis with pelvic ring displacement. And to organise a urologist as there could be internal damage. X-rays, of course, and scans, but the specialists will order what they want.'

The trip back was swift, Abed landing the small craft on the pad on the top of the hospital. As soon as the rotors slowed, a group of men rushed forward, opening the door, hauling out the stretcher and letting down its wheeled legs.

Gemma scrambled out, anxious to see no more harm came to Yusef in the transfer. She found the person who seemed to be in charge, and told him what she'd given Yusef, explaining that his self-diagnosis had been a broken pelvis.

'We'll take it from here,' the man assured Gemma, 'although you might like to come along with him. The X-rays and scans could be uncomfortable, he might like to have your support.'

Who did she think Gemma was? His lover?

Well, she was, but not officially—in fact, she'd turned down the official position. Gemma spun around, thinking Abed would be a far better person to be accompanying Yusef, but he was back in the helicopter, obviously about to take off, abandoning her at the hospital.

It seemed to take for ever, the scans, the discussions and consultations, different staff being brought in, male nurses to cut off Yusef's clothes, trusted lackeys moving in to shield him from prying eyes. And through it all, Gemma remained by his side. She had to, for his hand had grasped hers and wouldn't let it go, no matter how woozy he seemed to be.

So much for unseemliness, she thought at one stage. Now everyone in the country will know he's been carrying on with the red-haired foreigner. But she didn't leave him even when his hand dropped hers, or when she was asked to wait outside the X-ray room. She hovered close, determined to be there for him, whenever he needed her, unseemliness forgotten in worry and concern.

Although sadness filtered through as well, sadness that should she be the mistress, it would be the wife who was here beside him—more reason that her decision had been the right one.

'This ilium bone he's broken, is that serious?'

Abed had returned and after consultation with one of the specialists he'd turned to Gemma.

'Not as bad as some of the other bones in the pelvic ring, but he'll probably be off his feet for up to twelve weeks depending on where the break is. Maybe less if they are pinning it.'

'They are,' Abed told her. 'They're taking him straight from X-Ray to Theatre. They're prepping him—that is the word?—now.'

It's a straightforward operation, Gemma told herself, but fear for the man she loved had gathered in her mind and body and held her in its grasp. She thought of the important and powerful muscles that attached to the pelvic girdle and could only imagine the pain Yusef must have felt as he'd tried to drag himself back to the vehicle.

'I will take you back to the compound,' Abed said. 'The operation will be long, they tell me.'

Gemma frowned at him.

'Are you telling me I have to go—that I can't stay here at the hospital to see him when he comes out of Theatre?'

'Wouldn't it be best?' Abed said gently.

'Best for whom?' Gemma demanded. 'For him, so no one knows he's got this red-haired woman in his life? What about me? Where do I get a say in this? I love him, Abed, I want to be here with him, and if me staying here causes problems then he'll just have to get over them as best he can because I'm staying and I'll keep on staying until he tells me to go, okay?'

To Gemma's surprise, Abed laughed, and then he hugged her.

'I'll make sure there are English-speaking staff around so you can question them,' he said. 'And don't worry about publicity, the floor where he will be taken after the operation is sealed off from the public and the press.'

Abed departed, leaving Gemma totally confused. If Abed didn't want her to leave because of publicity, why had he suggested it? Because once Yusef came to his senses and was unaffected by drugs, *he* might not want Gemma around?

Well, too bad there as well, because she was staying.

He came out of Theatre five hours later. Gemma, who'd been shown to a small room where she'd dozed and leafed through magazines she couldn't read, was led into the recovery room, one so familiar it could have been in any hospital anywhere in the world. The anaesthetist was there, taking it on himself to stay with his important patient, and it was he who assured Gemma that the operation had gone well.

'Was there other internal damage?' she asked.

'Muscle involvement but nothing serious,' he assured her, then he nodded to where Yusef was stirring on the bed.

'Sit by him, take his hand, he is more likely to respond to you than to the voice of a nurse he doesn't know.'

'Even though I speak in English?' Gemma said, suddenly shy in front of this man and the three nursing staff in attendance.

'He has spoken English from his childhood, and it is your voice rather than the words that he will respond to.'

Gemma stared at the anaesthetist a moment longer, seeking any kind of judgement in his face, but he was nodding encouragingly and one of the nurses was holding a chair for Gemma by Yusef's bed, and she could read no condemnation in any of their faces.

Only concern, and maybe love, for she knew from talking to the women that Yusef was already loved as a ruler.

Though not by everyone! Someone had beaten him badly

and if it wasn't Hassim, who had it been? She'd been so concerned about Yusef's condition she hadn't thought to ask Abed what had happened—what he had found out.

She sank into the chair and took Yusef's hand, unable to stop herself touching his cheek where a dark bruise was now appearing.

'He was very lucky the physical damage was confined to his hip, the X-rays showed no skull fracture,' the anaesthetist was saying. 'Broken ribs, superficial cuts and bruises elsewhere, but nothing drastic.'

Though still watchful, he moved away, waving to the nurses to step back and give Gemma some privacy by the patient's side. Gemma held Yusef's hand and talked to him, reminding him of their meeting, which seemed like such a long time ago. Talking of the island, too, although uncertain whether he'd remember that day as good or bad. But it *had* been magical, so she recalled that magic, the rock fall with the ferns, the cool, clear water in which they'd swum.

He was swimming. The water was deep, deeper than he'd thought, but he was swimming upward, to the top. He had to get there, for Gemma was waiting for him, calling to him, needing him, she said.

Had it only been need, the thing he'd thought was magic?

It must have been because she wouldn't live with him.

Yet she was there, at the surface of the water, waiting for him…

He struggled, sank, struggled again, and finally said her name.

Or thought he did.

He must have said something for the fingers holding his had tightened, and he could hear her voice again.

'Gemma?'

He thought the word had come out stronger that time, but if he was still under water maybe she wouldn't hear, so he tried again, and this time he felt her hand on his cheek and pictured it, tiny golden freckles on the fingers, tiny pinpoints of delight.

'I'm here, Yusef,' she said, in case he hadn't recognised the hand. 'Can you hear me? Can you open your eyes?'

He tried but his eyelashes were stuck together.

Her fingers brushed across his eyelids, unsticking them, and he opened them to see her sitting by his side.

White walls, sheets, drip stands.

'Hospital?'

'You were injured, broke your pelvis, the bone's been pinned, you're just out of Theatre.'

A very concise explanation from the woman by his side, the woman who was clinging to his hand as if she'd never let it go. But what was *she* doing there?

Here?

He tried to make sense of it all but was too tired.

'Too tired,' he managed, by way of apology for not talking to her, then he drifted off to sleep.

'That's proper sleep,' the anaesthetist told Gemma. 'We'll keep him on the monitors here for another hour then shift him to a room. Do you want to stay?'

Try to shift me, she wanted to say but she stuck with a quiet but firm 'Yes, please.'

One of the nurses brought her tea and sandwiches, which Gemma looked at with surprise.

'It is easy food to have on hand in hospitals,' the nurse said, correctly guessing Gemma's reaction. 'We have them specially made for the hospital, for patients, guests and staff, a good supply. It is something that was recommended when the hospital was built.'

Gemma shook her head. The longer she was in this country, the more she was surprised, most often by the different customs but sometimes by strange innovations like a humble sandwich being available in the hospital.

One nurse remained to watch the monitor, but apart from her, Gemma was alone with the man she loved. Did he know that now? Was her presence by his side enough to tell him of her love?

And would it bother him?

She decided she no longer cared—no longer cared even about the mistress thing, coming to the conclusion that if that was all she could have of Yusef, maybe that would do.

Maybe…

But right now her main worry, when she wasn't worrying about Yusef's health, was what was happening beyond the hospital walls. Had Hassim grabbed the opportunity of Yusef being out of action to take control of the country?

Would Yusef's plans for the peaceful co-existence of the old and new settlers come crashing down? Would his desire that his people kept their old values be forgotten?

Sitting there, looking at Yusef's now so familiar face, her heart aching with her love for him, Gemma worried for him. At first she'd been suspicious of him, regarding him in the same light as her grandfather, a stern, authoritative man, but then she'd grown to know him and to understand the depth of his love for his country and its people. Now she worried for that country and those people, people she, too, was coming to love.

It was all too confusing and she was suddenly very, very tired, so she rested her head on the side of his bed and closed her eyes, drifting into an uneasy doze.

* * *

He felt better when he woke this time, and Yusef looked around, remembering the trip out to the desert, Hassim and Makka, falcons, then—

The next thing he could recall was Abed coming, a hazy recollection of a helicopter flight, scans, an operation. A nurse who'd been watching the monitor came towards him, asking if she could get him anything. A drink of some kind?

He shook his head, aware there was someone even closer than the nurse, and turned to see Gemma's head on the bed beside him. His right hand was clasped in hers and tucked under her head and now he was fully awake he suspected he had pins and needles in that hand.

But she was sleeping and it was such delight to watch her sleep he wouldn't—couldn't—move his hand.

The scarf she'd wound around her head had come askew so tendrils of red hair had escaped and were coiling around his hand, soft bonds tying him to her...

He lifted his left hand, wanting to touch her hair, her face, but it was tethered to the drip on that side and wouldn't reach, so he could only look at her, and wonder what magic conjunction of the fates had brought him and her together.

And that they would be together he had no doubts. Wasn't her presence by his side proof that she cared about him? Not to mention the flight she'd undertaken, for all her fear of flying.

Yet he'd shamed her by offering her an inferior position! He realised that now, although his thinking at the time had been that as his mistress she would be special—far more special, in his way of thinking, than a wife.

Though obviously she hadn't realised that. Had he mentioned love? Had he explained?

Of course he hadn't, thinking she'd be so overjoyed to be offered the position, her acceptance would be a mere formality.

Then doubts began to gather like dark clouds before a storm.

Was he reading too much into the rescue mission?

To her sleeping by his side?

He tried to puzzle it out, but his brain was still foggy and now it appeared they were going to move him and he'd have to wake her. He moved his hand and her head came up immediately, so he was looking straight into her eyes, her own bleary with sleep, but worried still.

'You're awake? Do you remember what happened? Do you know you've had an operation? You were right, it was your pelvis. They've pinned it.'

She was still holding tightly to his hand so he lifted it, and hers as well, and pressed their fingers, joined, to his lips.

'Hush,' he said. 'I remember what happened but you are not to concern yourself about that. I'm being moved now, but I don't want you exhausting yourself by staying at the hospital. I am doing well, although I imagine when the drugs wear off there will be pain, but I can get through that. You must rest, look after yourself.'

He was sending her away. Even through the fog of unrestful sleep Gemma knew that, but something deep inside her rebelled.

'I can rest here while you sleep,' she told him. 'You don't think I'm going to fly a rescue mission in one of those little sardine cans and then give up on my patient just because he's in hospital, do you?'

'And if I ask you to leave?' he said, and she straightened up and smiled at him.

'You'd have to do better than that, Your Highness,' she announced. 'You'd have to order me to leave.'

Then she clasped his hand again, and leaned forward to kiss him on the lips.

'I know you don't want my love, Yusef—you didn't ask for it—but you've got it. I don't know how it happened, but I fell in love with you, and, loving you, I'm staying with you until you're over the worst of the operation and out of the worst of your pain. I won't neglect my job, and Yanne will keep working on the project, but I'm staying here with you.'

'You love me?'

Yusef's voice was weak. Exhaustion or repudiation? But before Gemma could work it out he'd drifted back to sleep, leaving her sitting by his side, a red flush of embarrassment colouring her cheeks for not only had the nurse heard her declaration of love but the anaesthetist had returned in time to catch the gist of it.

The private room was palatial in its dimensions and its fittings. No hospital white here, the walls a rich crimson, the curtains gold, views out to the mountains from one window and to the sea from the other. Abed came shortly after Yusef had been moved, but his brother was asleep.

'Here,' he said, leading Gemma to a door and opening it to reveal another smaller room, and beyond it a bathroom. 'Family always come to hospitals with the patients,' he explained, 'so we have these suites where they can stay. I will get Miryam to pack some things for you and bring them here. Would you like her to stay as well?'

Gemma shook her head, still coming to terms with a hospital suite as lavish as this one.

'This,' Abed continued, 'is the button that you press to order meals, although once Yusef is ordering his own meals he can order for you.'

Yusef?

Gemma sighed.

'He told me not to stay,' she admitted, suddenly feeling not as brave as she had earlier. 'I argued but if it's going to upset him, having me here, maybe I shouldn't stay.'

'In your heart you must know what's best,' Abed told her, and Gemma sighed again.

'I know what's right in *my* heart,' she said crossly. 'It's what's in his heart that's the mystery.'

'Ah,' Abed said, 'who knows what is in another person's heart?'

And with that less than comforting comment he departed, leaving Gemma with the magazines she couldn't read and a man she loved sleeping off a major operation.

And she still hadn't asked Abed what had happened...

CHAPTER TWELVE

FOR two nights she stayed, talking to Yusef when he was awake, listening to his tales of his childhood, of falconry, and camel racing, and camping in the desert, even a little about his schooling in that strange cold land called England.

'It was to fit us for the new way of the world we were sent there,' he explained. 'To make us more able to fit into international politics, but people forget that one's own country must come first. If one can govern it with fairness and compassion then one will find one's place in the wider world.'

'You…' Gemma hesitated over the word but in the end settled for the rather pathetic 'discussed'. 'You discussed this with Hassim when you were out with the birds?'

Yusef grinned at her.

'Polite way of putting it but, yes, we did, and I thought it had been settled to the satisfaction of both of us.' He hesitated, then took Gemma's hand as if he needed support before he could say more. 'I had underestimated Makka's devotion to my brother. I had told them I would wait to see the sunset and he returned with three henchmen, to teach me not to steal from my brother—seeing my succession not as the gift of our eldest brother but as the theft of Hassim's birthright.'

'And now?' Gemma asked, and Yusef shrugged his shoulders.

'Now,' he said, 'I do not know what is happening beyond these walls for Abed keeps it from me, but neither do I care—well, not enough to keep me awake at night. Yes, I would like to continue to rule my country because I believe I have its best interests at heart, but I have made an even more important decision. I will no longer hide my feelings for you.'

He cupped his hand around her cheek.

'I love you, Gemma Murray, love you and want to marry you, and if that causes political upheaval then so be it, because no crown is worth the sacrifice of losing you.'

Gemma stared at him, unable to believe what she'd heard. Then she thought of all the ideas he had for developing his country, all the dreams he'd shared with her.

'That's nonsense,' she snapped. 'Shakespeare might have gone on about all being well lost for love, but you can't give up your country on a whim.'

'It is not a whim,' he said, and drew her closer so he could press a kiss against her lips. Then he lifted his head and looked into her eyes. 'Will you marry me?'

Would she?

She saw the love he spoke of in his face and felt it in the way his fingers trailed along her cheek, but to say yes, to deny this man his birthright just to satisfy her own longings to be with him? Was that right?

Now the fingers trailing down her cheek touched her lips.

'You don't have to answer straight away. Go back to the compound, have a proper sleep, walk in the rose garden, play with Fajella, think about it.'

She opened her lips to protest that she wanted to stay, but he closed them with another kiss.

'Go,' he said, and she heard the order in the word and remembered thinking—oh, so long ago—that he had the same cold authoritarian demeanour as her grandfather.

How wrong she'd been!

Her grandfather had given orders because he had been one hundred per cent certain his way was always right, while Yusef's orders, when he gave them, were for the good of the recipients.

Like now!

She left, her heart torn between love and duty. And if marrying her meant Yusef would lose his crown, then *her* duty was to refuse his offer—to head back to Australia just as soon as she could get on a flight.

Her body shuddered at the thought, but she knew she'd find the strength to do it.

Back at the compound, she was slipping into the guest house when the older woman, the woman Yusef spoke of as his father's senior wife, called to her from the loggia of the women's house.

'He is recovering well?' she asked, as Gemma came towards her and sank down on the top step.

Gemma nodded, uncertain how much of what had happened this woman would know. All of it, she suspected. Hadn't Yusef once said the women ran the households?

'Hassim is deeply troubled by what has happened,' the older woman said, and although she was about to nod, Gemma remembered Yusef's words back in the desert.

'He was not to blame,' she said, but the older woman shook her head.

'He is responsible for Makka's actions, he knows that, but also he knows that Yusef will make a better ruler because he has the ability to bring people together. As long as Hassim can do the business side of things, he is happy to let Yusef run the country. It was a—' she hesitated and Gemma realised this was the most English she'd ever heard the older woman use '— misconception on Makka's part that led to Yusef's injuries. Makka has left the country, you should know that, and leaving Hassim, that will hurt him more than any legal punishment.'

Gemma let the information sink in, then wondered why she was being told all this. To reassure her Yusef was safe, or perhaps to tell her Yusef's rule was assured and she, Gemma, shouldn't rock the boat.

She looked at the older woman, seeing the dark kohl-rimmed eyes studying her carefully.

'And where do I fit in?' Gemma asked.

The woman stood up, obviously preparing to walk away.

'You must look in your heart for that answer,' she said, and she slipped out of her sandals and disappeared through the always open door.

What was in her heart? Gemma knew the answer to that one. Love! So much love that she ached with it. But was love enough?

She returned to work, interviewing staff now, knowing that before long her time in Fajabal would be over.

Unless she married Yusef!

She thought of him, so high above her in the hospital, but stayed away, because being with him, seeing him, only strengthened her love and made her decision so much harder.

Then a summons came through a young nurse who looked a trifle scared but bravely delivered the message she had learned by heart.

'His Highness demands your presence,' she said, and dropped a little curtsey.

Gemma bit back an urge to tell the girl she could tell His Highness where to put his audience, and followed her along the corridors to the elevator foyer then up and up to the top floor.

And all the time her temper rose, mostly, she knew, from guilt that she hadn't been back to see him sooner, but also from fear because she knew he would demand an answer.

'You didn't have to send for me—I would have come,' she said, as she marched through the door, then she stopped dead for the hospital room had been transformed. Okay, so it hadn't looked that much like a hospital room to begin with, but now it was hung with draperies, rich silks and velvets, and Yusef's bed had become a kind of ottoman, covered in rich satin in gold and scarlet stripes.

And in the centre of it, he sat—well, maybe he was propped—clad in the snowy robes of his office but with a white cloak trimmed with gold over his gown, and a gold-trimmed cloth on his head, so utterly regal, so utterly magnificent, Gemma could only gape.

Yusef dismissed the nurse with a wave of his hand, and smiled to himself at the look of wonder on Gemma's face, but he hid the smile and kept what he hoped was a look of proper hauteur on his face.

'It takes you so long to consider the proposal of a king?' he demanded.

Gemma switched her attention from the trappings to him, and studied him for a moment.

'Will you still be a king?' she asked, and he frowned at her, for he'd suspected that had been the problem.

'Have I not told you that it doesn't matter?' he said. 'That I love you and if you love me that is enough.'

He heard her sigh and knew it had come from deep within her, then he chuckled and said, 'Come here.'

She drew close enough for him to grasp her hand, and once he had that, he could tug her near enough to kiss.

'This might not look entirely like a nomad tent,' he said,

'but I have taken us back in time, my love, to when it was traditional for a man to take the wife he wanted, throw her up in front of him on his camel, and ride off with her into the desert. Returning one week later, they were considered married and both tribes, his and hers, although they might have been warring, would accept this, for it was the way.'

She moved far enough from him to look into his face.

'Are you saying your people will accept our marriage? That your reign will not be threatened if you throw *me* up in front of you on your camel?'

He saw the hope in her eyes and heard it in her voice, and kissed her again, for the joy she brought to him was beyond words.

'My people,' he said, when she had been thoroughly kissed, 'so my spies tell me, will not only accept our marriage but will be delighted, for they see you as a red-haired heroine, a woman of spirit and courage worthy to be their queen.'

He watched the colour rise in her cheeks as it always did when she was embarrassed, and saw the golden freckles spark to life. But his spirited bride wasn't ready to submit just yet.

'You talk a lot of nonsense,' she said, her voice severe for all her eyes were dancing. 'And I haven't said I'd marry you.'

He smiled and tried another kiss.

'But that's the beauty of this way of doing things, you don't have to agree. Here we are galloping across the desert on a fleet-footed camel, you either go along with it or leap off.'

Gemma smiled at the image but she heard the note of strain in his voice and knew, although he was trying to keep things light, he was very, very anxious. But he'd put her through a lot of pain—mistress indeed!

'I might hurt myself if I jumped off,' she teased.

'All the more reason to stay on,' he said.

'And what about our week in the desert?' she persisted, poking him in the sternum. 'Are you up to that?'

He caught her to him once again, wincing as she fell against his bound ribs.

'Witch!' he murmured as he kissed her. 'You know full well our week in the desert is a long way off, but it will come, my beautiful Gemma, or maybe a week on our island, just the two of us.'

He tipped her head back and framed her face with his hands.

'Will you marry me?'

She nodded, and he shook his head.

'I need the words,' he said, 'need to hear them.'

'I will marry you,' Gemma told him, her heart hammering so loudly it was a wonder he could hear her.

'Say it again,' he ordered, and because some orders were worth obeying, she did.

'And again.'

She frowned at him.

'Three times and it's official,' he said, smiling at her be-musement. 'A very old custom, as old as the riding off on the camel one. Tell me three times and the marriage is sealed, although, my love, when I can walk again we'll have another wedding, one that all the people can enjoy and join in our celebrations.

Gemma sank down on the bed beside the man she loved, and now she took his face in her hands and looked deep into those dark eyes.

'I will marry you,' she said for the third time.

EPILOGUE

GEMMA was walking in the rose garden outside the women's centre at the hospital, Fajella skipping on ahead of her then coming back, patting Gemma's leg and asking 'You good?' every few minutes.

Because Gemma wasn't good, and lacked the stoicism of the Fajabalian women she'd seen give birth. Her labour pains, though still far apart, were harsh enough for her to know she'd probably scream and yell. Thank heavens she'd had the good sense to install a second birthing room in the women's centre, one with a deep bath and a shower so she could have warm water to ease her pain.

And one of the O and G specialists from the service was standing by, ready to assist, up to date with pain relief, even an epidural, should Gemma decide that's what she'd need to bring another Fajabalian royal into the world.

'Daddy come?' Fajella asked, and Gemma smiled at the little girl, amazed as ever at the ease with which she switched between the two languages, even having two names for her father.

'Not yet, precious,' Gemma told her, for she knew just how anxious Yusef was about this birth and she didn't want him knowing it was imminent until the last possible minute.

She supposed his anxiety was natural, having already lost one wife in childbirth, but he was a doctor, he knew this time it would be straightforward, so his fussing and anxiety were hard to understand.

'It's because I love you,' he said, only minutes later when he'd phoned her for the fourth time in three hours. 'And you're already two weeks overdue. You should have a Caesar, get the wretched child out of there. What's it doing? Waiting for some propitious conjunction of the stars?'

'Yusef,' Gemma said, hoping her voice alone might soothe him, 'everything will be all right.'

'Easy for you to say,' he muttered. 'You're not about to go into a meeting of the elders and argue for an increase in funding for education, and how can I concentrate on my arguments when I'm worrying about you the whole time?'

'Stop worrying,' she said, 'or send Abed to the meeting and go out in the boat.'

'And if you go into labour while I'm tacking against the wind, what kind of a husband would that make me?'

'One that's out of my hair,' Gemma said, then she disconnected for the next pain had come and she didn't want to be groaning into the phone.

'Come with me!' Yanne had appeared and she ushered Gemma in front of her, sending Fajella off with Anya, taking Gemma into the big bathroom of the clinic. 'Now, use this, show me how it helps,' she ordered, and Gemma smiled at the woman who had become her friend.

She stripped off her clothes while Yanne filled the bath with hot water, then Gemma slipped into it and immediately felt better, as weightlessness eased the pressure on her back, which ceased to ache with quite such persistence.

For another six hours she rode the pains, coming more frequently now. She walked with Yanne to support her when she could, seeking refuge now beneath the shower when the pains were strongest, rising with them to their peaks then feeling the relief as they eased.

'It's time to let Yusef know,' Yanne said, as the shadows lengthened in the courtyard, and the sun sank in the west.

And this time Gemma didn't argue, wanting Yusef with her, wanting to share the miracle of birth with the man she loved so dearly.

'I should have come before,' he told her, but when the pains came again and he saw her suffering he forgot to chide her, holding her instead, steadying her, encouraging her in the breathing they had practised together, suggesting pain relief, urging her to take it, growing angry at her refusal yet somehow understanding that it was important for her to deliver her baby as the women of Fajabel delivered theirs.

But they didn't wholly follow the old ways, for the baby boy was delivered by his father, sliding into the world and into his father's safe and loving hands, Yusef cradling the baby, his eyes full of wonder, the miracle of birth so deep and meaningful he couldn't speak.

Gently he laid the baby in his wife's arms and now he held them both, his arms cradling them as he looked in wonder at his son.

'He is so absurdly like you I feel cheated,' Gemma said, after examining the newborn for some time.

'Ah, but he is your child for sure,' Yusef argued, 'for he has arrived with little fuss, just efficiently and well, the way you handle all the situations in our lives.'

Then he kissed his wife and held back tears, wondering if life would ever be as good again as it was right now, in this moment, with his wife, his baby and his little daughter coming in to meet her brother.

Gemma remained in the compound for the forty days, and if she didn't cut off all contact with the women's centre, neither did she make her presence felt. She was there if she was needed, but mostly she spent the time with the baby and with Fajella, Yusef joining her each night because there was no way he was going to live apart from his wife and family for forty days.

But on the fortieth day they all climbed the high walls of the compound to a platform above the gate, where Yusef showed the world his son. Knowing the time was right, a huge crowd had gathered outside the compound, and the people yelled and laughed and clapped as Yusef held the baby aloft.

'Is it so great a thing, to have a baby?' Gemma asked, when they were back inside the house and the baby was sleeping after a feed.

'Babies are our future,' Yusef said. 'They are our guarantee that no matter how things change in our lives, the next generation will be there to steer the people through whatever lies ahead. But they are also a promise—a new birth of an age when things can get better, for shouldn't we always look to the future to be better?'

'That's a big responsibility for such a little babe,' Gemma said.

Yusef took her in his arms.

'I might have feared that once, but not now,' he said. 'When I think what you have achieved for my people, I know any child of yours will have the power to achieve anything he or she wishes. With us to guide him, with siblings and cousins and friends, our children will flourish, my Gemma, because on top of all we can give them in a physical sense, we will also give them love.'

'Love,' Gemma echoed, and felt her heart fill with it, for her love for Yusef grew with every breath she took. Love bound them together in a way she could never have guessed would happen, and love would see them safely through their lives together, however many little Akkedis they had.

MEDICAL™ 2-in-1

Coming next month

THE NURSE'S BROODING BOSS
by Laura Iding

Dr Brock Madison can't believe Elana Shultz works in his new A&E department! Even though she's a daily reminder of his troubled past, Brock simply wants to spend the rest of his life with this nurse in a million – if only Elana will let him in…

EMERGENCY DOCTOR AND CINDERELLA
by Melanie Milburne

When charismatic Eamon Chapman discovers the vulnerable beauty his co-worker Erin Taylor hides behind a prim and proper persona, he finds himself wanting to give this innocent doctor the fairytale happy-ever-after she truly deserves!

CITY SURGEON, SMALL TOWN MIRACLE
by Marion Lennox

Dr Maggie Croft's decision to have her late husband's baby has left her juggling pregnancy with the care of a small town community! Maggie can't afford any distractions, until the arrival of irresistibly gorgeous Max Ashton changes her mind…

BACHELOR DAD, GIRL NEXT DOOR
by Sharon Archer

When single dad Luke Daniels returns to Port Cavill, Dr Terri Mitchell remembers him all too well! Soon Terri has fallen for Luke and his young daughter, but can she convince this doctor to let her heal his troubled heart?

On sale 2nd April 2010

millsandboon.co.uk Community

Join Us!

The Community is the perfect place to meet and chat to kindred spirits who love books and reading as much as you do, but it's also the place to:

- Get the inside scoop from authors about their latest books
- Learn how to write a romance book with advice from our editors
- Help us to continue publishing the best in women's fiction
- Share your thoughts on the books we publish
- Befriend other users

Forums: Interact with each other as well as authors, editors and a whole host of other users worldwide.

Blogs: Every registered community member has their own blog to tell the world what they're up to and what's on their mind.

Book Challenge: We're aiming to read 5,000 books and have joined forces with The Reading Agency in our inaugural Book Challenge.

Profile Page: Showcase yourself and keep a record of your recent community activity.

Social Networking: We've added buttons at the end of every post to share via digg, Facebook, Google, Yahoo, technorati and de.licio.us.

www.millsandboon.co.uk

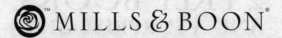

2 FREE BOOKS
AND A SURPRISE GIFT

We would like to take this opportunity to thank you for reading this Mills & Boon® book by offering you the chance to take TWO more specially selected books from the Medical™ series absolutely FREE! We're also making this offer to introduce you to the benefits of the Mills & Boon® Book Club™—

- **FREE home delivery**
- **FREE gifts and competitions**
- **FREE monthly Newsletter**
- **Exclusive Mills & Boon Book Club offers**
- **Books available before they're in the shops**

Accepting these FREE books and gift places you under no obligation to buy, you may cancel at any time, even after receiving your free books. Simply complete your details below and return the entire page to the address below. You don't even need a stamp!

YES Please send me 2 free Medical books and a surprise gift. I understand that unless you hear from me, I will receive 5 superb new stories every month including two 2-in-1 books priced at £4.99 each and a single book priced at £3.19, postage and packing free. I am under no obligation to purchase any books and may cancel my subscription at any time. The free books and gift will be mine to keep in any case.

Ms/Mrs/Miss/Mr _____ Initials _____

_____

Surname _____

Address _____

_____

_____ Postcode _____

Send this whole page to: Mills & Boon Book Club, Free Book Offer, FREEPOST NAT 10298, Richmond, TW9 1BR